Keep It Simple, Stupid

Peter Goldsworthy was born in Minlaton, South Australia, in 1951. He grew up in various country towns, finishing his schooling in Darwin. Since graduating in medicine from the University of Adelaide, he has devoted his time equally to medicine and writing. He is married to a fellow graduate and they have three children.

Peter Goldsworthy has published four collections of poetry, including *This Goes With That: Selected Poems 1970–1990* and *If, Then*. He is the author of four collections of short fiction, including *Little Deaths*, and four novels, including *Maestro*, *Honk If You Are Jesus* and *Wish*. He has recently written the libretto for the opera of Ray Lawler's play, *The Summer of the Seventeenth Doll*.

Keep It Simple, Stupid

PETER GOLDSWORTHY

flamingo

An imprint of HarperCollins*Publishers*

Flamingo
An imprint of HarperCollins *Publishers*, Australia

First published in Australia in 1996
by HarperCollins *Publishers* Pty Limited
ACN 009 913 517
A member of the HarperCollins *Publishers* (Australia) Pty Limited Group

HarperCollins*Publishers*
25 Ryde Road, Pymble, Sydney NSW 2073, Australia
31 View Road, Glenfield, Auckland 10, New Zealand
77–85 Fulham Palace Road, London W6 8JB, United Kingdom
Hazelton Lanes, 55 Avenue Road, Suite 2900, Toronto, Ontario, M5R 3L2
and 1995 Markham Road, Scarborough, Ontario, M1B 5M8, Canada
10 East 53rd Street, New York NY 10032, United States of America

National Library of Australia Cataloguing-in-Publication data:

Goldsworthy, Peter, 1951–.
  Keep it simple, stupid.
  ISBN 07322 57697.
  I. Title.
A823.3

Cover illustration by Annmarie Scott.
Cover design by Darian Causby.
Printed in Australia by Griffin Paperbacks, Adelaide

9 8 7 6 5 4 3 2 1
99 98 97 96

Acknowledgements

I would like to thank my editor Clare Forster for her tireless work. Christopher Pearson also offered his usual valuable insights at crucial stages in the growth of the manuscript.

Diana Cavuoto Glenn, of the Department of Italian, Flinders University, deserves special thanks for her creative input, not least of which was the correction of my Italian.

The usual gang offered their excellent support and suggestions: my wife Helen, daughters Anna and Alexandra, son Daniel, agent Tim Curnow, and at HarperCollins, Angelo Loukakis and Lisa Mills.

P. G.

Summer

1

He woke from the anaesthetic into a changed world. No one in the small, shared ward would talk to him. A pair of bulky headphones clamped the ears of his neighbour, a plump butcher with a bandaged left hand, a captive but willing audience for jokes the night before. Missing finger jokes included. Jokes about fingers and cleavers had caused the loudest laughter of all.

Floating on a cloud of drugs and pillows, Mack nodded, drowsily; the butcher promptly turned his back.

The two beds on the far side of the ward contained a pair of Berts, both with new metal hips, both carefully avoiding his eye. The larger studied a tiny personal television, unblinking; the smaller kept his head buried in a cumbersome, large print novel.

'Mayday, mayday — can anybody read me?'

No answer. Perhaps Mack only thought the words. Something uncomfortable filled his mouth — a tongue, his, an obstacle in the path of speech. His lids, still drowsy, drooped shut. When he forced them open another hour had passed. Fiona, the tiny day nurse, was rolling him over, roughly.

'Handle with care, Fiona.'

She yanked out the bottom sheet in one swift, angry movement. It might have been a tablecloth, and she was performing a trick, leaving the table setting undisturbed.

'Get out of the wrong side of the bed, Fiona?'

Her features were small and sharp, her mouth a tight, disapproving asterisk.

'If you say another word. If you say a *single* word.'

Fiona, also, had been friendly the night before: ticking boxes on the breakfast menu, unpacking his overnight bag. She had shaved his knee — The Knee — tenderly; pleased, he sensed, to have a youngish man for once in her care.

Young. Younger. Youngish. The declensions of middle age.

The operation had lasted an hour, but it might have been a year. It might have been twenty years. The world he had re-entered was changed, utterly.

Another fur-ball of words struggled past his tongue. 'Am I in the future, Fiona?'

The joke sank without trace; the nurse had vanished. Had he slept another hour between the intention to speak and the utterance? His heavy lids slipped shut yet again. A kiss brushed his lips; his wife was bending over him.

Lisa, also, was changed — but must have travelled back in time, growing younger. Her hair had turned bright orange; the nape was sharply shaven, a punkish flirtation. Her clothes matched the hair: short white socks, cloddish black school shoes, black skivvy. Thirty-five going on fifteen.

'Take me to your leader,' Mack mumbled. 'What planet *is* this?'

'New image,' she said, and stepped away from the bed to twirl, theatrically.

The butcher watched from the corners of his eyes; Fiona's bird-face peeped from the nursing bay.

'You were unconscious, Mack. It seemed a good time to spend money. You like?'

He did like. Something in the ironic clothes and cheeky cut of hair struck a chord.

'Weird,' he said.

'They grow on you. An acquired taste.'

'I'm still trying to acquire the last taste.'

She smiled, and this at least was unchanged in the future, a small warm sunburst. She slid into a chair at the side of the bed. 'So how are you?'

'Hungover. But it's nice to have someone to talk to. I seem to be in disgrace.'

She glanced about, curious. 'Have you been a naughty boy?'

'If only I had — it might be worth it.'

Her smile widened into a laugh. Grateful for the sound, grateful merely for a response, he reached for her hand. This, also, was unchanged, the same square handful of stumpy fingers and bitten-down nails. Ten Thumbs: an old, tender nickname. The flesh of her palm felt as warm as the glow of her smile; he suddenly wanted more of that comforting warmth pressed against him.

'Pull the curtain around.'

'You want to get yourself in more trouble?'

'I just want a little privacy.'

He took her hand and placed it beneath the sheet; she removed it.

'Can't stay, Mack. Have to go.'

'Already?'

She lifted the bedsheet further and examined his leg. It lay there like a bandaged log, like someone else's leg.

'How's the million-dollar knee?'

'The Club is paying,' he reminded her. 'It's all covered by insurance.'

'I don't mean the money, Mack. I mean is it *worth* it? You have to grow up sometime.'

'I like your outfit,' he said. 'You look about fifteen.'

She shrugged, caught out, and reached inside her shoulder bag and produced a thick, almost cubic paperback.

'Something to fill the time.'

'What — bricklaying?'

'Very funny. We did it last month in book club. You might just like it.'

'I haven't finished colouring in the last book you gave me.'

Her eyes looked a little glassy. 'I have to go, Mack.'

She rose and kissed him on the forehead, but he caught her hand again, and this time refused to release it.

'See you tonight?'

'I can't make it — curriculum meeting. Sorry. That's why I brought the book. But I'll see you in the morning. Okay?'

'Okay.'

'Once more with feeling.'

'Okay, for Christ's sake!'

She smiled again, that familiar small-wattage sun, tugged her hand free, and walked away in her cheeky, punkish clothes, watched by Mack's neighbours: three pursed mouths, six narrowed eyes.

The smile lingered in his memory, Cheshire-cat fashion, when all else — the blue eyes, slightly asymmetrical, the thin body in its silly clothes, the bitten nails — had faded. He lay on his bed with his eyes closed, made sentimental by his isolation, remembering the first time he had seen her smile, on a wintry mountain top. The memory itself was warming and comforting, a companion of sorts. They had found themselves in the same car after school that day, driving into the Hills, in a convoy of teachers. An impromptu expedition had set out from the staff room, drawn by the rumour of snow, a substance seen only on Christmas cards and cinema screens. Both Mack and Lisa were new to the school, their exchanges up to that point limited to social noises: time of day, weather information. And now the weather brought them together, like a polite conversation that had gotten completely out of hand. As Mack knelt on the summit of Mount Lofty, fingering the dirty slurry that bore no resemblance to the white stuff of fairy tales, a compacted lump of something that was half mud and half ice crunched into his back.

He had turned, and looked at her properly for the first time, the lips of her wide smile blue with cold, and known instantly that they would be lovers.

2

The hospital was small, private, newly redecorated; more an intimate hotel, at first glance. Pastel colour schemes predominated, cool cling-fruit flavours: apricot and peach. The nursing staff, women mostly, wore designer uniforms — flight-attendant uniforms — splashed with those same pastels.

Was the intention therapeutic? Perhaps there was something refreshing and calming about those soft colours, but the effect was transient on Mack. As the drugs leached from his system, he was restored to his normal restless, twitchy state of mind. The television offered temporary escape; he channel-hopped, but nothing caught his eye. He took up Lisa's paper brick, but read a few pages only, eyes on autopilot, seeing everything, absorbing nothing.

'It hasn't even got pictures,' he complained loudly.

No one was listening. Formal visiting hours began at seven. The ward filled quickly with various extended family clusters, curtains were tugged about beds, voices whispered and murmured.

From time to time a disapproving face peeped

through a curtain-gap in Mack's direction.

'Unclean!' he finally shouted, exasperated. 'Unclean!'

Vince Rossi arrived towards the end of visiting hours with a tube of *Baci*: chocolate kisses.

'On behalf of the committee, Mack.'

Mack didn't believe his old friend for a moment. 'Did the committee pay?'

Vince shrugged, an admission of sole responsibility. He opened one end of the tube, spilled the contents onto the bed, and unwrapped one for himself and one for Mack.

The silver foil wrappings contained little mottoes, lines from sentimental love poems mostly, in several languages.

'Kisses are the small change of love,' Vince read.

Mack peered down at his own wrapping. *'A good fuck is the large denomination,'* he intoned, solemnly.

'Bullshit,' Vince said, laughing. 'Let me see that!' But the wrapping was kept out of his reach.

'The chocolate never lies,' Mack told him.

Ritual complete, the men chewed silently for a time, completely at ease. They had played in the same team years before, Mack at the beginning of his career, Vince at the end of his. The younger player had depended on the older absolutely, off the field and on; a younger brother, of a kind, in the days when old Beppe Rossi, Club patriarch, had taken Mack under his wing.

Half street waif at the time, at odds with his own father, Mack had found a second home — *una seconda casa* — at the Club, and a weekend refuge at the Rossis' tiny half-house on Charles Street, a stone's throw distant.

'The Honorary Dago,' his father liked to sneer, but his duties were far from honorary. On weekends there was real money to be earnt on various Rossi & Sons building sites.

Food, also, could be earnt, in vast quantities.

'Too skinny,' Beppe would declare, nightly, prodding Mack's ribs or biceps. *'Un chiodo.'*

The old man was a Nail himself. Small and dark and lean, his body might have been bent from coathanger wire, indestructible as it hunched all day over bricks and tiles, mortar and grout. Tufts of hair poked from his ears and nose; his thick single eyebrow, a cartoon eyebrow, was shared equally by both eyes.

'Pelle e ossa,' he would warn, glaring out from under that eyebrow. Skin and bone. *'Metti su carne.'* Put on some meat.

What was Italian for the pot calling the kettle black? Beppe's wife, working night shift, was seldom seen at meal times, but his ancient mother, *nonna* of the congested household, issued those same warnings to her skinny, ageing son as she piled his plate with steaming mountains of rice and noodles and macaroni pie. Or so Mack guessed: her advice, in dialect, was

11

incomprehensible. He had learnt to follow, with difficulty, the compromise Italian of the Club, but the grandmother's long, loving consonants and lazy, swallowed vowel endings were beyond him. In her muttered 'grudz' he managed to find a *grazie* — but after that, nothing. She, of course, understood his pidgin perfectly, her ears sharpened by exposure to several versions of her mother tongue, among which his was just another, if more error prone.

'When do they let you out?' Vince mumbled through a mouthful of dark chocolate.

'Depends.'

Vince was taller than his immigrant father; good in the air as a player. He was wearing a business suit, and two-toned suede shoes of the kind Lisa liked to call brothel creepers. The suit was too small; since retiring from the game his tallness had evened out, width had begun to catch up with height. He'd become more square, or cubic — a solid six-footer. His shape was his mother's, from his father he had inherited nothing but an eyebrow, and a taste for chocolate. He unpeeled another before speaking. *Baci* were an old habit, or addiction: Beppe's favoured reward to his boys and players, a single *Bacio* for each scored goal.

'So what's going on around here, Mack?'

'What do you mean?'

'I asked for directions at the desk — some nurse. A

12

real spunk. Would have thought you'd have her eating out of your palm. But as soon as I mention your name …'

'I don't want to talk about it.'

'What?'

'The test result. I don't want to talk about it.'

Vince waited, expectant, his tongue stuck in the glue of chocolate. Mack stared him in the eye, unwavering.

'This won't go any further?'

'Of course not.'

'It's positive.'

'What test?'

'What test do you fucking think?'

Vince stared back at him, incredulous. No easy prey, he was thrown, momentarily. Some flaw in Mack's impassive mask told the truth; Vince's relieved half-laugh was followed by a reprimand.

'You had me worried, Mack. Jesus! Touch wood. What a crazy thing to say! You shouldn't joke about things like that.'

'Jokes are *for* things like that.'

'Seriously, Mack. Sometimes you're the life of the party. But sometimes you're just a pain in the arse. You never know when to stop.'

'Give us a kiss,' said Mack, loudly.

Vince glanced nervously towards the other beds, screened behind curtains, and quickly passed across another chocolate.

'You know what the old man would say. *Vai oltre i limiti*. And I mean *way* beyond the limits. No wonder no one will talk to you around here.'

3

'I hear you were pretty talkative, Mr McNeil.'

A clue. The night sister stood at Mack's bedside, shaking down a thermometer. Plumper and older than her day shift colleague, her nature also seemed more ample, less constrained. Her cheeks were deeply dimpled, the corners of her eyes finely creased. The form of her face had followed its functions; this was someone who laughed a lot.

'What do you mean?'

'Under the anaesthetic. You were pretty talkative.'

'How could I be talkative when I was asleep?'

She poked the glass tube beneath his tongue, a slim, bitter gag, tasting of antiseptic.

'Some people get a little … loose-tongued as they wake up.'

Another clue. Unable now to speak, he glanced about the ward, at the faces of his fellow patients, still studiously ignoring him. What exactly had he said?

She read his mind. 'Best not to repeat it.'

There was no disapproval in this older woman's face; a nursing sister of too many years' experience to be easily surprised or shocked. The lines of her face were an autobiography, in cuneiform script: Been There, Done That. She plucked the thermometer out, noted the reading, then began to unwrap the thick crepe cladding around his knee. Mack lifted his head from the pillow and watched, curious. The joint was swollen, a smooth, featureless balloon. Black sutures punctuated the thin pink scar, ants in Indian file, with raised antennae.

'No, tell me: what terrible things did I say?'

She dipped a sponge in some sort of black iodine solution and brushed the row of ants without answering.

'Damn?' he prompted. 'Darn?'

The corners of her mouth tightened, enigmatically, at the weak joke.

'Don't tell me,' he said, more relaxed. 'Let me guess. I took the Lord's name in vain?'

'Not even warm.'

'*Vaffanculo?*'

The obscenity failed to register, or translate.

'Maybe you're hiding something,' she teased. 'Maybe the anaesthetic was like some sort of truth serum.'

'Did I speak with *my* voice? Or did I sound possessed?'

'Sweet dreams,' she said, tiring of the exchange, and packed away her tray of shining, clattering tools.

The dreams when they came were more sour than sweet. Mack had spent too much time sleeping through

16

the day; the remnants of his usual sleep quota were doled out in small portions, fitfully, through the night. The disapproving Fiona was back on duty when he woke from the last of these, morning shift sunlight drenching the ward.

The bed next door was stripped and empty; the big butcher had vanished.

'He asked to be moved,' Fiona explained, brusquely.

'Why?'

Her mouth was still pursed, the muscles of her small face drawn tightly about it.

'You really have to ask?'

'Yes — I do.'

'Then you can ask *him*. He's in the next bay.'

The surgeon visited after a breakfast which contained none of the items he could remember Fiona ticking two nights before. A youngish non-communicative type, a whiz kid recommended by the Club, he shook and rattled the swollen knee joint for some time before murmuring various noises of approval, mostly to himself.

'The knee of a seventeen-year-old,' he mumbled. 'Even stronger than the undamaged knee …'

'So when can I go home?'

At this the surgeon lifted his head and spoke directly to his patient for the first time.

'Today. Crutches for two weeks. No weight bearing.'

This news was an enormous relief; frustration dissolved. A larrikin part of Mack — another seventeen-year-old part — reasserted itself. As Fiona sponged him, later, he felt bold enough to go on the offensive. He tried to imagine the worst things he could have said, the most shocking.

'Did I confess to fucking my dog?'

'You need to see a psychiatrist,' she said, and without warning took the bar of soap from her wash basin and jammed it hard between his parted lips.

His tongue still tasted faintly soapish when Lisa arrived to drive him home an hour later.

'So what was it all about?' she wanted to know, as the lift door shut out the ward and its hostility.

'Haven't a clue.'

She was examining the nail of her left middle finger, turning it this way and that, a prelude to further gnawing. She looked like a bitten finger herself, Mack thought, with her shorn punk hair.

'They must have said something.'

'Nothing.'

The lift door opened again, and Mack signed a small sheaf of discharge papers at the front desk. They walked out of the pastel air-conditioned hotel for the sick into the noise and crush of summer in the city, the madness of Christmas traffic, maddened further by the heat.

4

'You want to do *what*?'

Mack had been waiting some weeks to raise the matter, sneak it under Lisa's guard, ambush her. The moment seemed right. They lay together on the hard marble tiles of the bathroom floor — sole reservoir of coldness in a hot house — flushed, naked, still breathless, their bodies varnished with sweat.

'Buy a milk round,' he repeated.

Her hand, resting lightly on his chest, lifted clear; her thigh detached stickily from his.

'Is this one of your jokes, Paul?'

His given name, four-lettered, seldom used, had the force of an expletive.

'It's no joke. Sweetheart.'

'Buy a milk round with *what* exactly?'

Even at bathroom-floor level — a cooler, lower altitude — the summer heat was oppressive. It was far too hot for sex, although this, as always, only seemed obvious afterwards. Mack shifted his weight on the hard tiles: imported, Italian. The house, a cream-brick Rossi & Sons Dream Home, had been offered rent free, in lieu of match-payments: 'an offer we couldn't refuse', he liked to joke, defensively, to friends. 'The Display Home', was Lisa's version of the joke, equally defensive. Outside, the big brick box of the house was dwarfed by an even bigger entrance portico of white Roman columns, and a flight of marble stairs. Inside, the money had run out. The warren of low-ceilinged rooms seemed designed solely to store and magnify the summer heat.

'Okay,' he said. 'Not buy. Not yet. Lease the milk round for a few months. See how things go. *Then* maybe buy it.'

'Mack — you're going to be on crutches for a month.'

'I won't be rushing it.' He was still panting slightly, an overheated dog. The air, stifling, resistant, was difficult to inhale. 'I'll wait till the knee comes good.'

Lisa snorted. 'If!'

He shifted weight again, redistributing various bony pressure points. Discussion of the knee made him even more uncomfortable, reminding him of its presence, its constant stiffness.

'Sometimes I don't know who you *are* anymore.'

'I'm Paul.'

He immediately regretted the sarcasm, and made an effort to set the conversation back on track. 'It's Bruno's milk round.'

'Whose?'

'Bruno Panozzi. From the Club.'

'I haven't been to a game for months,' she reminded him.

'Big, with a crewcut. Smokes a lot of dope. You *must* know him. He knows you. Always falling asleep. Fell asleep at the Trophies Night. Fell asleep at the Dinner Dance …'

She was still shaking her head from side to side.

'I'll introduce you tonight. If he's awake.'

She resisted the joke. 'I haven't said I'm coming tonight.'

Her words struck some flinty surface inside him: another small flare of anger.

'Jesus, Lisa. I go to all your staff dinners. It's just a Christmas get-together, for Christ's sake. To meet the new coach. *All* the wives will be there.'

'How thrilling for them.'

The last piece of her anatomy still in contact with his — her foot — was withdrawn.

'You have something in common with those people, Mack. I don't.'

'You get on with Vince.'

'Vince gets on with *me*. God's gift to women. I have to constantly fight him off. He's a sleaze. I mean, those shoes — they say it all. There's no one to talk to, Mack.'

'Aldo's wife.'

'The Ladies' corner? No thank you!'

Lisa lay on her side on the cool, hard tiles, staring up at the ceiling, untouchable. Separated for most of each day by work and play, their conversations seemed to take place mostly in bed — or on various surrogate beds, the bathroom floor an occasional midsummer favourite. On such horizontal surfaces they still came face to face from time to time: flung together, husband and wife, by the usual need.

And also — mid-month, when the temperature of Lisa's ovulation chart crept upwards — by a colder, more calculated need.

'I take it you plan to give up teaching?'

'I thought … just for the year. Leave without pay.'

'But a *milk* round?'

Mack tried another joke. 'It could be worse. One of the fellas at the Club keeps fit working on the garbage trucks. Says he can find me a spot.'

'Please don't collect *our* garbage.'

'You don't want the neighbours to see?'

'I don't want my garbage spilled all over the street.'

Amusement at her own words flushed a little warmth into her voice; she turned to Mack and smiled for the first time.

'You've told Iain you might be leaving?'

'No hurry.'

'You don't think he has a right to know? As a

friend? He'll have to replace you.'

'If the knee comes good, I'll tell him in the new year.'

Her laugh was knowing. 'Keeping your options open?'

This was less question, than pronouncement. He wasn't serious, she had already decided. The milk round was a whim, another half-funny joke.

He tried to explain further. 'I have to do *something* physical. Every season it's harder to keep up. The only exercise I get is scraping chalk across a blackboard.'

'You train three times a week, Paul.'

That name again, four-lettered, plosive, as if she were expelling something.

'It's not enough. So many young kids are coming through. I'll be lucky to make the cut.'

'Perhaps your body is trying to tell you something.'

She pushed herself up from the floor, jerked a succession of tissues from a box by the basin, and wedged them between her thighs.

'We're going to be a long time dead,' he murmured.

'*What* did you say?'

He raised his voice. 'We're a long time dead.'

She spluttered, suppressing a laugh. 'That's very deep, Mack. Very deep.'

She stepped across him and into the shower, naked and glistening, her orange hair spiky with sweat. He

23

rolled onto his back to watch: the dimpled buttocks, the waist that he could still almost encircle with two hands. The edges and corners of her face had hardened and sharpened with the passing of the years, her mouth had become as capable of narrowing into a frown as widening into a smile, but the waist was as girlish as ever.

His own rise from the floor was more difficult: his knee, still bandaged, refused to flex. He ran the hot water tap, steaming, into the basin, plastered his face with a thick cladding of shaving foam, and began, carefully, to scrape away the white mask with his razor.

'Sculpture,' he said.

Her reply was muffled, drowned in the rush of water. 'Did you say something?'

'Shaving is like sculpture. You take a lump of soap each day, and carve out a new face.'

Her own face poked around the shower curtain. 'Pity you never seem to get it quite right.'

He laughed, and scraped on. The face that was emerging from the white mask might indeed be showing the signs of age, but his body continued to resist: endless hours of sport and weight training and even the daily physical jerks with the kids at school had seen to that. His body still felt, from his side, from inside, much the same: more sinew and gristle than flesh and muscle.

Il Chiodo, the older Members still remembered. The Nail.

He slid open the French doors and hopped through on his good leg. The air was no cooler outside, but a slight breeze tickled at his sweaty skin with an illusion of coolness. Other Dream Homes, in various stages of construction, patchworked the surrounding subdivision: timber frames, mostly, rib cages with neat cream cubes of bricks stacked about them, waiting. The Display Home alone was finished.

If nothing else, the view from Tuscan Heights — Wog Heights, in Club parlance — was good. Leaning on the hot rough stone of the balustrade, Mack gazed across the city plain. The flood lights of some distant sporting arena towered above the roof-line far to the west: four high light-towers, incandescent against the fading denim of the sky. Had pre-season training started, somewhere, already? The white glow tugged at him, twitched his leg muscles. Six weeks on crutches, another six of slow convalescence loomed large. He suddenly wanted to be down there under those lights, *doing* something: floating balls through the clear, summer air, zipping them precisely back and forth across the smooth turf.

Nothing had changed. He still couldn't walk past a couple of schoolboys kicking a ball around a park without joining in, a schoolboy himself, not too deep inside.

Lisa appeared in the open door, in summer punk: black singlet, ripped denim shorts. She was smiling again as she towelled her carrot-top, her tone conciliatory.

'What time are you due at the Club?'

'About half an hour ago. You've changed your mind?'

She shook her head. 'I'll drop you off. It's late night shopping, I need the car. A few last minute ideas. You can get a lift home?'

'I can always hop.'

5

'Science,' the new coach barked, and paused, liking the sound of it, his first public utterance at the Club.

Mack arrived in time for the speeches, on crutches, his knee swaddled in a bulky bandage. Outside, the heat was beginning to dissipate, but the squat brick blockhouse, packed with sweating men, felt like a sauna.

The coach, Billy Colby, stood on a raised platform at the far end of the long room, a yappy fox terrier with a sharp nose, and teeth pointing in several different directions. He was encased in a Club tracksuit: the red, white and green *tricolore*. It looked several sizes too big, a hand-me-down. Aldo Rossi, older brother of Vince, and Club Chairman again since the last committee-room coup, stood at his side.

'Modern football is about science, lads.'

The accents were English. A Liverpool voice, Lennon and McCartney, but without the perky humour and self-mockery. There was something pinched and malnourished about the shrunken face and crooked teeth. Or so it seemed to Mack, keen to find fault. Platters of prosciutto, melon, olives and pickled

27

vegetables surrounded the players; he was tempted to suggest that the new coach should be eating, not talking.

A blackboard had been set up at Colby's side; his chalk squeaked across it.

MODERN FOOTBALL = SCIENCE.

Aldo Rossi nodded sagely, but down in the ranks there were murmurs of boredom, or discontent. Someone rolled an eight-ball silently, pointlessly, across the blue pool table.

The coach glared from his raised podium, a new Headmaster on his first Speech Night. The text of that glare was clear: Don't Speak Unless Spoken To. No one said a word. No one breathed. Even the pool ball found a pocket and hid. Each player knew exactly the powers invested in that cocky bantam figure. Impositions and detentions. Fines for non-attendance at training, endless laps and push-ups for those who were slow out of the change rooms. Expulsions, Suspensions. The Bench, on match days.

And, always, the terrible sword above each head: Failing To Make The Cut.

For those who could live within these constraints, or threats, the Club provided well: more kindergarten than school, cosseting its players, showering them with gifts, making decisions on their behalf, allowing them, above all, not to have to grow up.

'Discipline,' the coach added, and chalked up the word, misspelt. DISIPLINE.

A couple of the committee members up front — Vince Rossi, Equipment Officer; Gino Trimboli, Club Trainer — exchanged glances. There had been mutters over Colby's appointment: the first coach in Club history with no Italian pedigree. Down in the ranks minds were wandering; bored, overheated players glanced here and there, some in search of food or cold beer, others seeking out the reassurance of their own faces in the gallery of fly-flecked team photographs from past seasons that hung from the brick walls. The low tin roof seemed to act as a kind of lens, focusing and magnifying the heat; the air was a thick soup of sweat, cheap aftershave and the rich fatty aroma of grilling meat from the barbecue outside. Paper streamers and Christmas decorations hung motionless from the ceiling. The fans that hummed, straining, in the background, seemed unable to budge the heavy air.

TACTICS, Colby added, his chalk squeaking painfully.

'A football team is a body. The players are the limbs.'

Bruno Panozzi, team captain, reached across the bar and refilled his glass from the beer tap.

'You!' Colby called sharply.

Bruno was still facing backwards, waiting for his beer.

'You. Panozzo, isn't it? Where is the team's brain?'

Bruno turned slowly; a big man, head and shoulders above the crowd, possibly even at eye-level with little Colby on his podium.

'It sure ain't here,' he said.

The room erupted, but Colby's face remained set. He chalked a crude stick-figure on the board as he waited for the laughter to die.

COACH, he scrawled inside the circle head, and tapped the word several times with his piece of chalk.

'Here,' he said. 'The coach is the team's brain.'

A few last snorted laughs could be heard; he glared around, seeking them out.

Mack, oldest of the assembled players, was helping himself to a piece of dry, stiff prosciutto from the nearest platter. Three beers on an empty stomach had clouded his head; he needed some sort of antidote: a food-sponge to dilute the effects. His movement caught the coach's eye.

'You don't agree, McNeil?'

The chalk was aimed Mack's way, a white gun barrel; his mouth was crammed too full to answer.

'Careful,' Bruno warned, in a whisper. '*È pieno di pepe.* He's full of pepper.'

Colby's glare intensified. 'You have something else to say, Panozzo?'

Mack rescued his team mate, forcing out an answer

through the tough, stale ham. 'He said, would I like some pepper.'

A ripple of sniggers spread through the room.

Colby raised his voice a notch. 'And *I* said, you don't agree that the coach is the brain of a team?'

Mack swallowed the wad of ham, with difficulty. 'Seems to me the problem this season might be where the heart is.'

Another ripple of sniggers. The committee members who surrounded the podium maintained fixed smiles, barely.

Aldo Rossi stepped forward. Much the same height as Colby, he was darker and more thickset. And better dressed. No Club tracksuit for Aldo, and no two-toned shoes; his suits were imported, Milanese *alta moda*. He looked worried, trying hard to find a joke to defuse things.

'Seems to me you're more worried where the stomach is, Mack,' he offered.

Laughter filled the room again; even the English fox terrier in his outsized tracksuit managed a small, crooked-toothed grin.

Aldo pressed on, rallying the players. 'We had our critics last season, gentlemen. A coupla players — we won't mention names, they're not worth mentioning — said things in public. Some won't be back, they know why. Others — well, I hope they learn their lesson.'

He paused, making eye contact here and there.

'What was said — I'm not going into it here — was lies. This Club is open to everyone. Italians *and* foreigners.'

He paused, acknowledging the laughter.

'There are no secret rules about certain nationalities on the team. Mack McNeil can tell you that: a player who's been with the Club for years. Right, Mack?'

'Sì!' Mack called from the back. *'Per mia sfortuna.'*

The laughter of the members was followed by a second, delayed burst from the non-Italians as Aldo translated. 'Unfortunately for him.'

He waited for the laughter to die, then pressed on. 'We even allow Greeks to play for us.'

More laughter; the Zervos brothers grinned from a corner.

'We've brought Billy Colby here to win promotion, gentlemen. And ladies. A few people — again, we won't mention names — have said we got a second division mentality. Too many years out of the heat. Billy is here to prove that wrong. Billy Colby is a winner. Every club he's been, he's won a championship.'

Aldo Rossi, master salesman, in full flight, selling morale instead of Dream Homes. Perhaps the laughter lulled Mack into believing that anything could be said, under cover of banter. Perhaps it was the beer, loosening his tongue. He drained his glass and muttered softly:

'But why has he been to so many?'

Bruno and a few others within earshot laughed.

'Didn't catch that up here, Mack,' Aldo called.

'Just a joke.'

Aldo was feeling pleased with himself, expansive, generous. 'No — go ahead. Please. Share it with the rest of us. We always enjoy your little jokes.'

'I said, why has he been to so many?'

This time no one laughed, especially not those who had laughed before. The silence held for a moment, then Colby smiled, thin-lipped.

'There's a joker in every pack. I'm looking forward to coaching you, McNeil. I think you and me are going to have a very interesting year together.'

Bruno turned and winked. 'Don't think the new boss likes you, Mack.'

The hot room emptied quickly. The Social Committee, wives of Members, had been busy outside; the aroma of grilling sausages and steaks and neat rows of chevapchichi and mounds of brownly transparent onion rings dragged the players by the nose through the doors. Even the malnourished Colby at last seemed interested in food; he stepped down from the podium and moved towards the door, flanked by Club officials.

'Mack — can't you ever keep the mouth shut?' Aldo whispered as he passed, but tolerantly.

Close up, there was too much of his late father in

Aldo for Mack to dislike him. *Due gocce d'acqua*: two drops of water. At times it seemed as if old Beppe — loved by Mack as much as he had loved anyone — had been resurrected. The son's skin was his father's: Arab-dark, burnt. The tufts of thick hair that poked from his shirt-collar and cuffs were his father's. Of course the single eyebrow was his father's.

Three inches lower, that eyebrow would have made a fine moustache, Mack as a boy had told a laughing Beppe. He had never risked the joke with the elder son, hiding inside his silk-ties and tailored suits, a southerner, a *terrone*, it seemed to Mack.

A single, high, flood light was burning at one end of the pitch, a few kids were kicking balls into the net in the dim light. The air, at last, was cooler, the sky to the west a vast wall of pink and blue stained glass, abstract in design, fast fading. The hubbub inside the Club rooms hushed into something quieter, more reverential, as the men moved outside onto the grass, lowering their voices as if entering a church. Or perhaps it was nothing more than different acoustics: there were no walls to amplify the noise.

Mack grabbed a beer and a plateful of food and joined Bruno on the highest steps of the stand, dragging his bandaged leg behind him. The Gang of Two, the previous coach had christened the two veteran players.

'You never fucking learn, Mack. One of these days.'

'Did the little bastard good. You've got to let them know early who's boss.'

Bruno shook his broad head, a thick medicine ball, unconvinced. 'How to win friends and influence people — not.'

The two men sat in silence for a time, sipping beer, sucking awkwardly at the leaking ends of too-thick sausage sandwiches. They had done no running, but there was an after-training feel to the night, the camaraderie of a session of hard work dissolving in the pleasant haze of alcohol. And, shortly, in other drugs: Bruno took a small press-seal plastic bag from his pocket, and rolled a lumpy, drooping cigarette, one-handed.

'Smoke, mate?'

Mack waved the offer away. 'I'm trying to get fit.'

High-pitched shouting and laughter carried from the goal-mouth as the ball cannoned among the children's legs. Two water sprinklers crawled along opposite sides of the pitch, casting long, chuttering arcs across the grass as the boys chased their ball in and out, screaming, revelling in the cold and wet. One or two were familiar to Mack from gym classes at school, but it was the single girl among them, smaller and thinner than the boys, who caught his eye: shielding the ball easily when it fell at her feet, sidestepping through the cluster of bodies, her long pony-tail flapping and bobbing.

35

Bruno distracted him. 'Here's trouble.'

Colby was approaching, climbing two or three steps at a time, a little man with something big to prove.

'Nice night,' he said, and settled himself onto a neighbouring plank, beer in hand, as if all that had taken place inside the Club rooms hadn't happened, as if he were suddenly just another player, a private soldier again, one of the boys.

'I wanted to get you two alone,' he murmured, after sipping.

Beer-froth left a thin white moustache on the rim of his upper lip; Mack half-hoped it would stay there, untouched, all night. As if somehow aware of it — an officer's neat moustache — Colby reverted to rank again.

'A team needs leadership,' he began. 'On and off the field. I expect the senior players to provide it.'

'We're not *that* fucking senior,' Mack said, lightly.

Colby ignored him. 'It's a young team. A lot of young lads coming through. I expect you two to set an example.'

Being on the receiving end of this felt strange to Mack, and was feeling stranger every year: being spoken to in the same tone of voice he used himself, all day, every day, to his students.

'I also expect a little respect. You respect me, I'll respect you.'

He wiped away his foam moustache, and once again the rank that went with it.

'We're all in this together,' he grinned, toothily. He turned his attention to Mack's bandage. 'How's the leg?'

'Tuscany doesn't look too good.'

Bruno laughed obligingly. An old Club joke: Beppe's Anatomy of the Leg. Half geography teacher, half football coach, the old man always described the leg by *regioni*: Rome of course at the knee-cap, Tuscany the thigh, Naples the shin, the stiletto-heel of Puglia.

The ball had been Sicily. *Naturalmente.*

'Is that some sort of in-joke, McNeil?'

'Just the local lingo.'

Colby ignored this. 'It's months since the season finished. Why did you leave it so long?'

'I'm a teacher. Had to wait till the Christmas break.'

'So when will you be fit?'

'Full training in March. Might miss the first few games.'

At this the coach rose and smiled, but without warmth. 'They're never the same after surgery.'

'Vaffanculo!' Bruno muttered, quietly.

'And up your arse, too,' Mack added, as Colby moved down the steps, out of earshot.

A wet, glistening soccer ball deflected upwards and out of the small pack of children playing in the sprinklers, bouncing all the way to the foot of the stand.

Colby stepped neatly over the ball, ignoring the call of the kids, and continued back towards the drinks table, glass in hand.

'Typical,' Bruno said.

Mack rose and hopped, stiff-kneed, down the steps to retrieve the ball. The beer had left him a little unsteady; he gripped the handrail for support. The girl detached herself from the group at the goal-mouth simultaneously; Mack reached the bottom step and, balanced on the splinted leg, side-footed the ball across the narrowing turf — a few yards now — between them. The soft instep of the foot: Basilicata. As she deftly flipped up the moving ball with her toes and caught it, he realised, suddenly, that she was in fact a he: the long hair and lean build had confused him.

'You've got good balance,' he said.

The boy stood, waiting for more praise, or to be dismissed. He was soaked: a smoky sort of steam eddied from his wet hair and sodden clothes into the warm night. Backlit, he appeared to be smouldering, about to burst into flame. His face shone with sweat or sprinkler-water, his T-shirt clung, translucent, to his skinny rib cage, a perfect mould.

Another Nail.

'Keep practising,' he called, as the boy abruptly turned away.

Mack hopped back up the steps and the two men

watched the children's game in silence. At a distance, in the dim light, the boy was little more than a rat-tail of wet hair and two long, bony legs, scissoring and lunging.

'She's not bad,' Bruno said. 'For a girl. Should sign her up. How old is she?'

'She's a he.'

As if reminded of the existence of women in the world, even, in this case, illusory women, Bruno turned the talk to Lisa.

'How's the missus?'

'She's fine.'

'Haven't seen her around the Club lately.'

'She's developed an allergy to the game.'

'They get like that. You told her yet?'

Mack occupied his mouth with another sip of beer, not wanting to be reminded, and not wanting to answer. But Bruno was not about to go away.

'Told her yesterday,' he finally admitted.

'And?'

'Still a bit of work to be done.'

6

The off-season passed too slowly for Mack. A week after the last match of September he longed to have a ball again at his feet. He craved the physical release of the games — the deep, addictive oblivion — but he also missed the hard, chubby face of the round ball itself, the way it would rub and bump against his toes, flip playfully from foot to foot, from chest to thigh to brow and back again. Obedience, reliability — these were the trusty virtues of a tightly-pumped soccer ball. *Fido*, in a word: faithful. Properly instructed, the ball could be taught to heel or lie or wait, to move on straight or curved paths, even, deftly underspun, made to return over short distances, as if on some invisible leash.

Simply, he missed his dog.

The long school break magnified his boredom. The previous summer he and Lisa had squandered the savings of eight years on eight weeks in Europe. The trip had been part holiday, part therapy: Lisa's miscarriage, her first pregnancy after some years of trying, had left her devastated. The famous smile had not been seen for weeks on end, and she lacked the energy even for the most simple household tasks. Eight weeks abroad meant two months, two further menstrual bleeds, cruel reminders of the earlier terrible bleed. Both had caught Mack unprepared and uncomprehending; he had sat on the edge of a hotel bed holding her hand, supplying tissues and stock consolations for the best part of the first day of each period. *We can try again. It's not the end of the world. Don't bottle it up. Get it out of your system.*

Between these two setbacks, Lisa had done her best, and slowly regained her old verve. Mack had filled her days — her two months — with a sequence of cathedrals and galleries and leaning towers and canals, all of them in Italy, the winter proving too cold on the other side of the Alps. He even managed, one freezing afternoon, to drag her to the Stadio San Siro, in Milan, to watch Baggio and Maldini and company at work in their vast office. These regular daily schedules and goals of travel also offered therapy for him: an escape from the usual summer restlessness, a continual deferral of his boredom. Now, back home, broke, and trapped, ironically, in a local outpost of Italy, he roamed the house at night and on weekends. A Kid on Holidays, Lisa teased, with Nothing to Do. Or perhaps he was a Tom Cat, with too much to do.

'You men are all the same. Can't bear to be shut inside. Why not get out in the garden?'

'On crutches?'

'You need the exercise.'

'You women are all the same.'

'What do you mean?'

'Can't bear not to nag men.'

'Very funny.'

In summers past he had escaped into the odd game of squash or golf with friends — Iain Davies from school, Vince from the Club — but there was an unsatisfying irregularity to these, a dependence on the timetables of others. Incapacitated, he found the long summer days even longer. Each morning he slept late, then sat in state in front of the television through the afternoon, a caliph on a reclining throne, ennobled, if only temporarily, by disability. Lisa set beer or food at his side, and tennis players and cricketers and Christmas carollers paraded all day before him, as if paying court, acknowledged or dismissed at the touch of a remote control.

'You know who you remind me of, Mack?'

Mack knew immediately, but wasn't prepared to admit it.

'Remember the first time I came home to meet him?' Lisa continued. 'Sitting in the backyard in his singlet, scratching his back. All you need is that ivory back-scratcher.' She laughed, but Mack could find no humour in any comparison with his father.

'There's one difference,' he said. 'My disability is genuine.'

Lisa reproached him, mildly: 'He did *die*.'

'Only after a lifetime of bullshit. Classic case of cry wolf.'

His father's throne had been an ancient, weather-beaten armchair, planted in the backyard, next to the pigeon loft. The old fraud spent each summer stuck fast to that ruined chair, sipping beer and sleeping. And scratching his back. And also, twice a day, studying his birds through a pair of binoculars as they wheeled high above.

He could pick his favourite blue or grizzle from miles away by the dip of a wing or bill, or its position in the flock.

'He loved his pigeons,' Lisa said, less to find virtue in the father than to calm the son, to discourage bitter talk.

'He loved them when they *won*. Otherwise he ate them.' He laughed harshly; it was her turn not to be amused.

'I remember their coop,' she said. 'It was like a palace!'

'It had to be. They had to *want* to return.'

Mack's job had been the scraping out of the loft each day. He would hand the gleanings to his father, and wait for feeding instructions as the invalid studied the lustrous tufts of down, or stirred the birdshit like porridge with his forefinger.

'Wheat and peas. Sixty–forty.'

His father's winter throne-room was the kitchen, and his scrutiny was turned back on himself. He sat by the warmth of the stove from dawn each morning, poring over medical textbooks, his lips moving methodically as he read. A 'Returned Man' — his self-description — and a war service pensioner, he knew more about disability than any doctor. He'd spent longer studying than any doctor; he could bamboozle any doctor.

'He *was* your father, Mack.'

'Could have fooled me. Bring us another beer, luv.'

His words might once have earnt a smile. Now they were too close to home. Had he in fact become the father he parodied? *Gocce d'acqua?* He tried to refute the connection, to distinguish between identical drops.

'Funny thing about the old man — after a few beers all signs of disability vanished. He left his walking stick at the pub every pension night. Didn't seem to need it anymore.'

She nodded in the direction of the crushed, empty cans at his elbow. 'Doesn't seem to help you.'

'I've only just started.'

In fact, he was trying to drink less, to at least defer his first beer till noon. He had set up his bench and weights outside on the terrace, and would spend each morning in exercise. Squats proved impossible, but he could bench press without strain. Biceps curls were also possible; he sweated out his restlessness in endless sets and repetitions. These at least inserted a firmer spine in the loose shape of the days, a reminder of the strict winter routines of training three nights a week, and Saturday games. There was also pleasure in the exhausted aftermath: the glow of muscles heated from within, an internal incandescence, which paradoxically, at the same time felt oddly anaesthetised — a numb heat. His arms and chest might have been rubbed with heat balm, a menthol or camphor liniment.

Most nights he slept poorly, waking in the small hours feeling empty, or perhaps less empty than unfilled, a turned-inside-out feeling that was difficult to describe, and because it was difficult to describe, difficult to acknowledge.

Lisa was often out: visiting friends, Christmas shopping, attending her book club, or watching movies with friends. Her hours at home were spent mostly in the garden. She had no emotional investment in this particular garden — neither of them had the slightest intention of inhabiting the Display Home any longer than financially necessary — but she enjoyed the processes and routines of gardening.

On Christmas Eve her temperature chart began to rise. She was reading in bed when he emerged, hopping, from the bathroom. The room was in shadow; her bed lamp shaded by a pink silk scarf. Her pillowed head glowed in the muted pink light: familiar invitations, sexual signals, arousing an automatic response.

What began on autopilot continued on autopilot, the dictates of the thermometer giving an over-clinical feel to their love-making, a hospital feel, as if they were the subject of some sort of fertility study, watched through mirrored glass by a team of clinicians. Lisa's responses were subdued, business-like.

'You don't like doing it with a cripple? It's supposed to be a turn-on.'

'It was fine,' she said, and kissed him on the lips, if only to hush his jokes, then turned away to sleep.

She woke him in the morning with another kiss, and Christmas greetings.

'Who have *you* been dreaming about?'

He rose and examined himself in the mirror. The evidence of a night of perpetual motion stared back at him: bloated eyes, wildly dishevelled hair. He could remember one fast-fading dream only. He had been writing school reports, had run out of ink, and had filled his fountain pen with tomato chutney.

Lisa laughed at the story, but offered no interpretation.

'I didn't talk in my sleep?' he asked, still looking for clues. 'I didn't confess to any murders?'

Sitting on the bed, amid the crumbs of breakfast, they exchanged gifts. Shirts and socks and compact discs passed in one direction, salad bowl and books in the other. All had been bought by Lisa. His acceptance of her offer to choose her own presents had disappointed her; too late he realised that she had harboured a hope that he would make a special effort, hobbling from boutique to boutique, on crutches. He tried to make a game of the unwrapping, to at least give the gift of humour. There were laughs to be milked from the fact that he hadn't a clue what he was giving her, but not many.

'Just what I always wanted to give you!'

The last parcel she handed in his direction was shoe-box size, a shape that was neither CD nor shirt. He stripped away several onion-layers of crepe paper, and lifted the lid to reveal a pair of shining, black soccer boots: Italian, imported, chamois leather, moulded soles.

He beamed, astonished and delighted, then lifted the open box to his nose and inhaled deeply, eyes closed.

She laughed. 'I hope they're the right size, Mack. I took in your old boots.'

He threaded a long lace carefully and repeatedly through the eyelets of the left boot, stretched the mouth, and slipped it over his foot. It fitted like a glove, which it was, of sorts. A foot-glove. He methodically tightened each rung of the laces, then tied and bound the boot. The long leather tongue lolled back over the laces, giving the boot the look of a panting, black-tongued dog. He wriggled his toes: the soft leather was so pliant that the press of each was separate and distinct.

'You could paint foot-paintings with these on your feet!'

Lisa laughed. Encouraged, he joked again.

'You could play the piano with these on your feet!'

'Don't get carried away, Mack. I get the point — I done good.'

'You done *terrific!* You could play blindfold in these.'

'Let's not make a fetish of it.'

'Can I wear them when we make love?'

'That depends where.'

He laughed. There was a playfulness in her words, a spontaneity that had been absent the night before. But he knew not to press: her sexual life was temperature-controlled, a thermostat.

'What did you get for Mum?'

As soon as he had uttered the words he regretted them; they provided a focus for her own earlier, unspoken, disappointment. A smile was still playing about her lips, but there was a new sharpness in her words. 'What did *you* get for her?'

'You usually organise it.'

'She's your mother, Mack. Even if you haven't seen her for weeks.'

'It's not that long.'

He strained, remembering, but of course she was right: from Day One of marriage she had kept a tally of such things. And remembered the birthdays, bought the Christmas gifts. Her training for this was better than his, or he had assumed it was. Marriage had allowed his memory to erase all redundant birthdates, faintly engraved at the best of times. To his shame he couldn't even remember his mother's birthday anymore, exactly. August, yes — the big print was indelible — but which day?

'Relax, Mack. I've got her some perfumed soaps. Native wildflowers.'

'I haven't exactly been mobile.'

'How many times did you visit when you had two legs?'

She knelt at the base of the tree and began packing the various family gifts into a basket. He could have given an answer, counted back and come up with a plausible figure — but if it wasn't the quantity of visits, it would be the quality.

'I hate going there.'

These words he also regretted the moment they left his mouth.

'You hate *going* there? What do you think it's like to *live* there?'

He had no excuse: he drove past the nursing home each time he visited the Club.

'You only ever think of yourself, Paul. More and more. You used to at least *try*.'

The real issue was less his neglect of his mother than his neglect of his wife. She paused, struggling with herself, perhaps regretting her words too. She had clearly wanted the morning to be special, to meet its seasonal quota of peace and goodwill, but there were things pent inside, too long unsaid.

'You'd think your knee would make you more sensitive to the problems of others — but no. You live in your own little world. Nothing else matters.'

Once commenced, the accusations now came in a rush, like segments of a train, each dragging out another by some obsessive logic of association.

'You're so … selfish. You either love something, or you don't do it. And you don't love much at *all*. What you love is — yourself!'

How could her mood change so quickly? She paused to gnaw at a finger, giving him time to speak.

'It's *you* who've changed. I haven't changed.'

'Maybe,' she said. 'Maybe I've grown up.'

'And I haven't?'

'You *are* just like your father. Totally self-obsessed.'

She rose, and vanished through the door. He could hear her in the kitchen, banging cupboards, opening and shutting drawers. When she returned he was puzzled to see a plastic measuring jug in her hand.

'You told me once he used to measure his piss every day — jot down the total in a notebook.'

She tossed the jug onto the bed.

'Here's another Christmas present. Because that's what you do. That's *you!*'

She walked through into the bathroom and turned on the shower. Mack lay on the bed, wearing nothing but his new soccer boots, stunned that she had remembered the anecdote, a forgotten joke at his father's expense, and stored it away to use, years later, against him.

7

The pale Christmas Day sky seemed bleached by the heat, devoid of blueness — an amorphous glare. Mack sat beside his wife, in silence, as she drove at snail's pace through streets jammed with big family cars packed with children and gifts. The congestion and the heat had destroyed all trace of Christmas spirit: horns blared, brakes squealed, drivers shouted abuse through open windows. A police car, slewed sideways, blocked the lanes on Regency Road. Waved on after a short delay, Lisa steered cautiously through an intersection carpeted with broken glass. Red and amber tail light fragments were spread across the bitumen like colourful Christmas decorations. Tow trucks surrounded a mangled car like predatory mantids, their gantries raised as if in prayer, but not for the victims, praying only that they would get the business. A police woman scribbled notes on a pad as she spoke to a young man sitting on a nearby fence, nursing his ribs.

'Season of donor organs,' Mack murmured.

A joke, as always, seemed the best peace offering.

'Maybe someone could donate you a new knee,'

Lisa said, her tone ambiguous, no easier to interpret than her silence had been.

The car climbed the Regency Road railway bridge, then coasted down into the vast flatness of the western suburbs. From the summit of the bridge, there was an especially flattened look to the squat houses and low roof angles of Regal Park, as if a square mile of the city had been heavily rolled. Bonsai homes, and bonsai trees: even the scrubby street vegetation seemed unable to venture above shrub height. The houses — red and grey-brick boxes, post-war welfare housing — had a hard-edged, doll-like simplicity, a lack of variety in design that at a distance, even after forty years of individual wear and tear and renovation, still gave the suburb the feel of a model development set up on a town planner's table.

Successive waves of immigration had washed through the Parks, giving and taking. The English — the Poms — had beached first, mixing easily with the local population of workers, pensioners, Returned Men and war widows. Next had come the Italians and Greeks, the Balts and Serbs and Croats, then the Lebanese, each wave washing the previous onwards and upwards into more affluent suburbs. Now the Parks were mostly Vietnamese. Hanson Street was a long mile of Asian groceries and eateries and Vietnamese video libraries and shopfront doctors with names like Ng and

Tran and Dang. Names that sounded like dropped cutlery, Mack's father had liked to joke. Over the years he had identified them all: Krauts, Balts, Dagoes, Wogs, Wops, Chinks — each label was a Proper Noun, exactly defined, and representing some precise geographic region, like a colour on a map.

Of post-war Little Italy, only the Napoli Soccer Club now remained, an acre of park between William and Charles streets. Of pre-war Australia only the street names remained. A block further back was George, then Edward, James, Henry. Running across the kings at right angles were the English queens: Anne, Mary, Elizabeth, a promiscuous grid in which each queen intersected with each available king and vice versa.

A former Boys' Home, and a frequent threat used against Mack throughout childhood, the Edward Street Nursing Home now housed only senile delinquents, a last refuge for the local war widows and the widows of workers, most of whom could now remember neither war nor husband. On Christmas Day some, at least, of the beds were empty, their occupants reclaimed by their children for a few hours of grace, but the staff was also on skeleton roster, and the handful of aides in their grubby grey uniforms looked as harried and overworked as ever. Those inmates — the word demanded its own use — not granted day-leave still cried for help, repetitively and without hope, from beds barred like cages, or chattered nonsense from wheelchairs.

Even worse, for Mack, was the familiar stink: a nauseous mix of incontinent shit and sickly sweet room-deodorant.

'Shoot me before I get to this,' he murmured, hopping after Lisa, on crutches, down the wide corridor.

The tone of her answer was still hard to pick, perhaps half-thawed: 'Keep playing soccer and it'll be sooner than you think.'

He clumped on past a series of open doors. Like a triptych of paintings in some gallery of medieval horrors, each of the first three doors they passed framed a different glimpse of the inferno. Mack averted his eyes from the force-spooning of mashed food into one unwilling mouth, then averted them again as he passed the next door, and a similar substance, texture and colour indistinguishable, was wiped by an attendant as it emerged from the other end of another inmate, only partly screened from public view.

The third door revealed an emaciated woman lying immobile in a high-barred bed. Her toothless mouth was open, her eyes fixed. She might have been dead but for the noise: a periodic high-pitched shriek, piercing in intensity.

'King parrot,' Mack said.

No reaction from Lisa, several steps ahead.

'Or maybe rainbow lorikeet.'

'Don't try so hard, Mack. It wasn't funny the first time.'

He lumbered on in her wake, reduced to the status of Try Hard, lowest rung in the schoolyard hierarchy. The fourth door was shut. MRS BERYL MCNEIL. Lisa knocked and entered, Mack followed on his crutches, awkwardly. His mother was slumped in an armchair, chin cushioned on her ample bosom, asleep. All the furnishings which had previously filled the small half-house on William Street were now crammed into this single room, it seemed to Mack. And in much the same geometric configuration, as if the walls of the house had merely shrunk, squeezing everything closer together.

The bed was Nursing Home standard issue, an aluminium frame jammed against the wall where an oxygen outlet, Nurse Call alarm, and a tiny, plastic thermometer cup were attached.

She roused herself at the touch of his lips, squinting. 'Hello, dear. I thought he'd forgotten.'

The words were aimed at her daughter-in-law, not at her son; she was incapable of criticising Mack directly. If the laying of blame became unavoidable, she would usually manage to take it upon her own bent shoulders. The familiar furnishings had perhaps helped preserve her mind, earthed it in memories. Surrounded by vacant minds, she at least could speak, and think, and remember.

Lisa bent and pecked her cheek. 'The traffic was terrible, Mum.'

'I'm sorry,' she said, accepting responsibility even for this.

'So you should be,' Mack murmured.

His approach to his mother was as oblique as her reproach of him. He disliked examining her closely. Most of her body was hidden, but what he could see always disturbed him in ways that he couldn't properly explain. Her lower legs had a swollen, mottled hardness to them — 'bad veins' — but higher up, especially in the arms and neck, the weight was looser. Her flesh hung on her arms like overly big sleeves. The sight was unattractive, yes — but it stirred something disproportionate in him, an immense squeamishness.

'I haven't seen Mack for so long. I should have rung.'

Once again she was speaking to her daughter-in-law, sharing the blame for her son's neglect.

'It's been difficult — with his injury.'

'We shouldn't let him play, dear. He's getting too old for it. '

Lisa caught his eye behind his mother's back: an exasperated Help Me.

He said: 'There's a lot of traffic on the road, Mum. I think we should get started.'

8

The streets around the cemetery were packed with parked cars; Lisa dropped the two invalids at the cemetery gates and drove on, in search of a slot. Mack, on crutches, and his mother, walking with the aid of a clacking, quadrupedal walking frame, proceeded awkwardly down the main aisle, between rows of headstones. Her gait was six-legged, a heavy-bodied insect; he was more a grasshopper with a pair of stiff, overgrown legs. The day was warm; his mother, sweating and breathless, needed frequent rests. Her bent back, as she hunched over the cumbersome aluminium frame, reminded him of the wing-case of a beetle.

'I'm sorry it's so hot, dear.'

'Just don't let it happen again,' he said.

He had once tried to re-educate her with such ironies; now he uttered them merely to entertain others. Or, if no others were present, for his own entertainment. He was still able to amuse himself. A small plastic bucket of weeding implements dangled from the cross-strut of her frame: hand-trowel, fork, gardening gloves. At the grave she released her support and knelt, laboriously — to garden, not to pray. High pepper trees shaded this section of the cemetery. The granite headstone was encrusted with hardened birdshit, as if splashed with white paint. She began to abrade the stains with a rag, beginning with the inscription: her late husband's name and dates, and a minimal Bible quote.

Come unto Him all ye that are heavy laden, and He will give ye rest.

Heavy laden: a good euphemism, Mack thought. The lower half of the stone was blank, reserved for her own final numbers.

'I should come more often. They don't seem to take any care.'

'It's hardly going to bother the old man, Mum.'

'It's all I can do for him. I think we should at least make the effort.'

Mack held his peace, with difficulty. The emotional glues that still bound her to her dead husband were beyond his comprehension. He had always been immune to the standard defences she would chant. *The War Changed Him. He Wasn't The Same Man. He Saw Things …*

Familiar refrains, these, from those pension days in his childhood when the house grew suddenly dangerous, and she would urge him quietly through the back door and into the car.

'Your father's not himself. He needs to be alone.'

At times she tried to spread the blame from the father to the son. 'He's so like you, Paul. Can you see that? Too much energy.'

As she drove he would sneakily examine her bruises. If she noticed, she would spread the blame even further, from the War, and from him, to herself.

'It looks worse than it is.'

'You know I bruise easily, dear.'

'I only have to *touch* something.'

She never sought refuge with her numerous sisters; unable to admit any problem to herself, she could hardly confide in others. Sometimes she drove as far as Norton Summit or Mount Lofty. More often she would settle for lower vantage points, parking the car on Windy Point, or some high roadside verge in Skye.

'Keep still,' she would murmur as she stared out over the neat, glittering lights of the city. 'Stop fidgeting.'

She was talking as much to her husband as to her restless son. Somewhere down there he was falling asleep; soon it would be safe to return.

Now, kneeling at the cemetery, she passed up the plastic bucket.

'I'm sorry to ask, dear. Can you manage?'

Mack clumped off to join the queue at the nearest tap, some distance away. Despite the crutches, and the bucket of water, he took the long route back, through the newest suburbs of the cemetery. Here the simple white headstones and minimal biographies — a life contracted to a name and two dates and a place — gave way to more flamboyant architecture, and more expansive inscriptions. Dream Homes, at least in scale: black marble sarcophagi, or booths of basalt and granite topped by ornate stone madonnas and carved angels and crucified Christs. The most luxurious of these final resting places were true mansions: the family mausolea. Their facades displayed sun-bleached photographs of the loved ones, some enamelled, others encased in ancient rusting frames. Personal details were inscribed into the stone, extracts from songs and poems, messages of love and hope.

The Rossi family plot was one of the most prominent. *Alla cara memoria di Giuseppe Salvatore Rossi, Reggio Calabria.* The words were chiselled in gilt on a black marble slab. *Nato 15.1.1913 R.C. Morto 2.10.1980 Adelaide. Padre amatissimo di Aldo e Vincenzo …*

A photograph inside a casing of clear hard plastic was affixed to the headstone: an unsmiling immigrant in a best suit, his eyebrow deeply furrowed, concentrating on the serious business of being photographed. It might have been Aldo in his worst suit, a chip off the old block. A *goccia d'acqua.*

The weight of the slab seemed far too great and disproportionate for the tiny figure of Beppe — an unnecessary mass of ballast, or retardant. But then the old man had always seemed indestructible. Whatever new illness or affliction had been dealt him, he fought back, tough as gristle. A year-long series of strokes, each an extension of the last, had slowly stripped the old man of his senses, but he had resisted to the end. The size of that immoveable slab amused Mack. Unable to destroy Beppe from the inside, Death had been forced to mount an attack from the outside, pressing him permanently into the ground.

His amusement seemed to liberate other, opposite emotions. The memory of that tiny, busy figure, felt hat jammed to eyebrow level, could still bring a lump to his throat.

'Riposa in pace,' he murmured, and felt an absurd urge to kneel and kiss the polished marble, as if a more flamboyant body language went with the spoken. Old *Baci* sayings floated back to him. *The heart has no wrinkles. A kiss makes the heart young again, and wipes out the years.*

Beneath the pepper trees, the women had scrubbed his father's headstone free of bird paint, and were raking the surrounding gravel.

'I spent the night here once,' he announced as he approached. 'When I was about ten.'

Lisa glanced up at him; even after eight years of marriage, he was pleased to note, she was still susceptible to surprise.

'Why?'

'It was a kind of dare. With myself. I wanted to prove something.'

'Did you?'

'Not quite what I intended.'

His mother stopped gardening to listen. 'I don't remember it, dear.'

'That's because you didn't know. I sneaked out through the window one night. A full moon.'

A late night movie had seeded the notion: *Night of the Living Dead*, or some such. Erupting graves, zombies shoving their heads up through the earth like bizarre vegetables.

His mother puzzled at the idea, unable to explain it to herself. 'You stayed the *whole* night?'

'It was a dare,' he repeated, as if that was sufficient answer.

Lisa was amused. 'Boys will be boys.'

'I wanted to know I could do it. Sleep all night on a grave. I didn't even take my sleeping bag. That would have made it too easy. I could have hidden inside the bag.'

She laughed out loud at this. 'A sleeping bag is spook-proof?'

'It feels safer. You know — snug.'

His mother was worried by particulars. 'Whose grave did you sleep on?'

'I forget the name. Over there somewhere. The oldest I could find. It had cracks in it — sort of collapsed inwards. Very sinister.'

Lisa shivered, involuntarily. 'What happened?'

'Nothing happened. Morning happened. The sun came up. I went home. End of story.'

He bent and removed last year's flowers — a clutch of dried, crumbling stalks — from the porcelain pot, and filled the pot with water from his bucket.

'I don't think he should have slept on a grave without asking permission, do you dear? He should have slept on someone he knew …'

Lisa turned away from the question, shaking with suppressed laughter.

'I couldn't sleep here, Mum. The old man wasn't *dead* yet.'

His mother flinched as if struck, as if the word was a rock. For once, she criticised him directly. 'I don't think you should speak like that, Paul. Not here. You should show some respect.'

'I never learnt respect.'

She held his eyes for a moment — talking to him, yes, but also for once actually seeing him.

'You shouldn't judge him, dear. You only ever knew part of him.'

Her tone was mild again, but something in her words gave him pause, some new thoughtfulness. One of her stock phrases stirred briefly in his mind, and dusted itself off. *The War Changed Him*. Leaning on one crutch, he reached down for his mother's elbow, and guided her to her feet, more tenderly than usual.

'Time to go, Mum. You know what Lisa's parents are like. Presents at noon. Turkey on the table at one sharp …'

'You forgot the Christmas pudding,' Lisa said, supporting the other elbow, fully restored to good humour.

'Pudding at two,' he said. 'Sharp.'

He flexed his arm theatrically, freeing his watch from the cuff of his shirt. 'Synchronise watches!'

9

Mack's timings were out by seconds rather than by minutes. Last to arrive, they found the champagne had already been uncorked. Lisa's parents Jenny and Don, her brothers Nigel and Terry, and their wives Margo and Jill, were encamped in a circle of chairs in the lounge room, sipping steadily. Margo's new baby was feeding from a liberated breast, while various older children sat or flopped on the floor, staring intently at the big baskets of brightly wrapped gifts which surrounded the base of the Christmas tree.

After a round of kisses and baby-noises, Lisa added her own basket to the collection. Her late arrival brought no recriminations: Mack's crutches and his mother's walking frame provided a self-evident excuse.

'I think we should make a start, Donald,' Jenny, the matriarch, announced.

A small, prim woman, a former nursing sister, her hair was pulled into a bun as tight as a grenade. She was the perfect match for her husband, a dapper architect in a blue blazer. They might have been twins. The sons, lawyers, were bigger and looser in shape, a pair of cuckoos towering over their parents, but both had chosen wives that were clones of their small, neat mother.

'Is that me, too?' Mack once joked to Lisa. 'You married me because I look like your mother?'

She had smacked her forehead. 'Of course — that's it! I never could understand what I saw in you …'

She had never been close to her big brothers or their compact wives; both couples lived interstate, and were seen no more than once a year. She took a formal interest in the children, sending parcels of baby clothes on each new arrival, and yearly birthday packages thereafter. Photographs of the nieces and nephews were clamped to the fridge door at home, held by magnets. Reminder notes, Mack privately thought of them.

She plucked the baby from its mother and perched it, gurgling, on her own lap. Put it back, he wanted to say. Put it in a basket under the tree. Give it to someone else. Those baskets were emptying fast; the children, acting as runners, ferried each gift to its designated recipient, or ripped eagerly at the wrapping of their own.

'This is for Ben — from Auntie Lisa.'

'Thanks, Auntie Lisa!'

'*And* from Uncle Paul,' Lisa insisted, again.

Mack had no objection to such omissions; Lisa had chosen and wrapped each gift. But there was a disproportion in the giving that irked him. As the children multiplied, it grew each year: Mack and Lisa, childless, gave much more than they received.

When he had raised the subject with Lisa on Christmas Eve she merely laughed.

'If you want more gifts, sweetheart, you only have to ask!'

'It's not that. It's just, they take it for granted ...'

'*You* could be a runner,' she interrupted, still laughing, 'you could hand *out* the gifts! Would you like that?'

Was the child in him jealous? Perhaps, but he also felt an injustice on her behalf. He resented the kindness of her sisters-in-law, the charity with which they offered their babies to her to be held and cuddled. He resented their unspoken pity. To Lisa he said nothing of this, for fear of sensitising her further, or damaging whatever psychological bulkheads she had in place. Talking could only make it worse, he felt — a reminder, a harking back that etched the hurt more deeply. Talking was a sort of menstrual period: a reliving of the grief that *became* the grief.

'Mum — it doesn't *work!*'

'Try the batteries the other way, darling.'

'But I like *hers* better than mine.'

Mack was largely immune to his nieces and nephews. He found them hard to tell apart, like

Chinese: their identical, big snow-capped heads, fresh faces, gap-toothed smiles. Fifteen years of teaching had tired him of the race of children: their sameness, their predictability. By the time the talk, as it always did over the turkey, turned to the latest cute sayings or precocious feats of the children, he was bored more than irritated. Even Lisa seemed to fall silent as her sisters-in-law directed their reminiscences mostly at each other, or at Mack's mother, an enthusiastic listener, always ready with the right refrain.

'Time for the family concert,' Jenny announced over the pudding, glancing at the watch, pinned, upside down, to her breast.

Beginning at three sharp, niece after nephew banged out *Für Elise* on the piano, or scraped tuneless minuets on toy violins, or blew strange disconnected sounds out through the holes of flutes.

'She's only been learning for two years.'

'Perfect pitch, his teacher says.'

After the concert, an impromptu obstacle race developed around the big dining table between two of the nephews, one using the crutches, the other the aluminium walking frame. Both grandparents were in the kitchen, preparing port and coffee; the four doting parents smiled proudly as their boys clattered noisily among the antique furnishings.

'They never slow down,' Margo murmured, fondly.

Mack saw the corners of his mother's mouth twitch, wanting perhaps to apologise in advance for any damage, but unsure of her position in this big, strange house. He had no such scruples. He ordered both delinquents in his sternest Phys Ed voice to down tools, pronto.

'Do what your Uncle Paul says,' Margo said, after a short, shocked silence.

'I should have folded it away,' Mack's mother said. 'I'm sorry.'

10

Lisa arranged a small get-together on New Year's Eve: a 'meal' for a handful of friends, rather than a party. Was it also intended as a session of group therapy for Mack? Her plans had a medicinal, therapeutic sound to them.

'You need company. Sitting around feeling sorry for yourself. Drinking on your own.'

There was also the matter of the milk round, still unresolved.

'If you're serious, you *have* to tell Iain.'

'Plenty of time.'

'It's not fair, Mack. After all he's done for you.'

'What's he done? He's got me teaching arithmetic!'

'Is that his fault? At least he gives you *some* time outdoors. It's more than you'd get in any other school.'

Lisa's boss, Anthea Pridmore, Junior School Head at Girls Grammar, arrived first, with flowers, red and white carnations. Iain Davies and his wife Mary, followed shortly, with wine, rosé and sauvignon blanc. The five friends sat outside on the terrace, sipping cold wine in the balmy evening, chatting without effort. All five knew each other well, perhaps too well; within the small, curved universe of the teaching profession all paths intersected, sooner or later.

Mack's intended career change was the main topic.

'So you're finally getting rid of him,' Anthea said to Iain.

'Couldn't take any more.'

The joke only half-concealed a deeper truth. Iain had shown no surprise at the news. Mack realised, sadly, that his friend was secretly pleased to have him out of his administrative hair.

Anthea turned to Mack, or perhaps on him. 'But why a milk round?'

He was leaning back, his folding chair balanced precariously on its back legs, teetering. He said, falsetto: 'It's something I always wanted to be, Miss Pridmore. When I grew up.'

The sun had slipped into the distant gulf; the surrounding foothills, covered in bush, and the suburbs below, the leafy Volvo Belt of the city, had a fine, grey, powdery look in the last light. Mack was reminded, oddly, of the close-packed contents that spilled from the dust-bag when he emptied the vacuum cleaner each Sunday morning. Darkness had infiltrated the verandah as the friends sat talking, their faces had lost definition, but Mack could still hear Anthea, even when she wasn't speaking. A hippie in her student days, festooned with beads and bangles, her jewellery had moved upmarket, become more conservative — but still she jangled softly each time she moved.

Lisa defended her husband. 'Mack needs to be physically busy. He'll never change. Gets bored and fidgety if he's not doing something. He's unbearable over summer.'

All eyes were on him, balanced absurdly on his chair. 'Look — no hands,' he wanted to shout, the words on the tip of his loosening tongue. Lisa deflected the conversation into a range of hot topics: global warming, Amazon deforestation. Mack had noticed this before: she would move from personal anxieties — childlessness, finances, him — into public events, her private fears magnified into universal cataclysms.

'It must be worrying to bring children into a world like this,' she murmured to Mary, mother of four.

'Leave the world out of it,' Mary said. 'They're enough worry themselves.'

Mack tipped down another wine. His tongue was altering its shape with each mouthful, dissolving in his mouth like a lozenge.

'I want the simple life,' he announced, more loudly than intended, reclaiming the conversation.

'I would have thought you were simple enough,' Anthea said.

He laughed. 'I've been thinking about it. I want to become less responsible.'

'You mean irresponsible.'

Her words came with a smile, but she was spoiling for a fight, Mack sensed. Since outgrowing her ex-husband three years before — 'outgrowing' was Lisa's verb, but a direct quote from Anthea, surely — Mack had been appointed Representative Male Shit.

'You always sound like a headmistress when you talk to me,' he said. 'Why is that?'

'Because you always sound like a little boy?'

The others laughed; even Mack grinned with grudging respect. Pleased with her answer, Anthea pressed on.

'You don't want to grow up. You want to be a little boy forever.'

'I wish!'

His words, uttered with some force, were sufficient propulsion to topple his teetering chair backwards. It collapsed beneath him.

'Bring him a high-chair,' Iain said.

More laughter. The various gold clasps and bracelets on Anthea's arms tinkled like wind-chimes.

Lisa, unsmiling, rose and began bringing out the food instead — bowls of iced gazpacho.

'Can I help?' Anthea asked, but without moving; staring instead at Mack, making a point. Another F in his report card. She often took the role of marriage commissar, less trying to improve him, he felt, than reprove him, or reveal his selfish male heart to his blinkered wife. He stared back, allowing Lisa to ferry out a tureen and five soup bowls alone, three separate trips. Anthea brought out the worst in him, especially when he was drinking; he played up, or down, to her expectations.

'Delicious soup,' she murmured.

'Mack made it.'

He had hoped this small fact would not emerge, preferring to shock Anthea rather than to please her. Above all, he didn't want her to think him capable of being improved — or, if he was improved, that she had played any part in it. She could believe what she wanted to believe. This had never been his deliberate strategy — more a self-entertainment — but it had a strategic benefit. In the contest for Lisa's approval that often developed, to out-bitch the Best Friend had proved useful in the past. Anthea also revealed a deeper, less pleasant self — and the depth of a hostility to Mack that otherwise went over Lisa's head.

'It's nothing,' he said. 'A few tomatoes chucked in the blender. I leave the cooking to Lisa.'

Lisa looked up at him, surprised.

'I can't get into all that women's business,' he said, his speech increasingly slurred.

Anthea was smiling, a Told-You-So smile. She returned to their earlier disagreement. 'This milkman thing. How long do you think you'll last?'

'Needs to apply himself,' he muttered, *sotto voce*. 'Disruptive in class.'

Iain said, 'We didn't catch that, Mack.'

'Who knows how long? I've managed to last in teaching for fifteen years.'

'It's hardly the same thing,' Anthea said.

'Isn't it?'

'Now, children,' Lisa warned.

'Of *course* it isn't the same thing. How can you even compare the two?'

Lisa persisted. 'Let him go, Anthea. He's finally found a job doing what he likes best — running around in circles.'

'At least I'm getting a little fucking exercise.'

Lisa glared, but there was no heat in his words. Or none intended: the adjective — fucking — seemed to help rhythmically, it was necessary to maintain the flow of his sentences. Especially when he was having a little trouble wrapping his tongue around those sentences.

'At school I'm not allowed to *do* what I was trained to fucking do.'

Mary spoke up for her husband. 'It's not Iain's fault.'

Mack waved an airy hand. 'No offence. I know you're on a tight budget.'

Iain had a contented gift-wrapped look about him: a round, plump parcel of corduroy, tied neatly at the neck with a colourful bow tie. He was never without that token flamboyancy. Mack had once spotted him mowing the lawn on a Sunday morning, in a green bow tie. Plain Ian at Teachers' College, the extra vowel had also come to seem a type of bow tie, a touch of colour, mildly attention-seeking.

He spread his palms. 'If it were up to me, Mack.'

'Pontius fucking Pilate.'

'Hey — I'm on your side,' Iain protested, good-humouredly.

Their friendship had stood the test of time, but episodically, depending mostly on geographic proximity. Their paths had criss-crossed over the years, through a sequence of school postings and promotions — but neither made an effort.

Iain suddenly tested the limits of that friendship. 'Haven't you had enough to drink?'

'You're right,' Mack said, also good-humouredly, and splashed more wine into his glass. 'I haven't.'

'It's past your bedtime,' Anthea told him.

He was being attacked from all sides. 'Can't I stay up, Miss Pridmore?' he whined. 'Oh, pl-e-ease. Just this once. Just a little longer.'

She smiled, reluctantly amused by his foolery. Lisa was less forgiving, later. Midnight had come and gone, various combinations of kisses had been exchanged, even between Mack and Anthea. Hands were held, auld–acquaintance unforgotten — and almost immediately, ceremony complete, the guests had vanished.

She sat at the bedroom dressing table, brushing her hair with quick, angry strokes.

'You used to be funny, Paul. Now you're just coarse.'

He bristled. 'I've heard worse from your mouth.'

'It's not just the language. It's a different voice. As if you're a different *person*. Especially when you're drinking.'

He pressed the toes of his left foot hard on the heel of his right sneaker and tugged the foot free, too weary and too drunk to bend and unlace. Too weary, also, to argue as Lisa continued, her brushstrokes emphatic, moving in time with her words, like a harsh rhythmic poetry.

'You should *listen* to yourself on the phone. I can tell who you're *talking* to by your tone. Listen next time one of your mates from the Club rings up. Fucking *this*, dickhead *that*.'

He freed the other foot from its sneaker and tugged his T-shirt over his head.

'That's how we speak where I come from.'

'Then maybe it's time to out*grow* it.'

That word again, outgrow, like a piece of grit, a contaminant.

He escaped into the shower cubicle, drowning any

further accusations in the noisy rush of water. Revived by the massage of those steaming fingers, he felt better, or at least more sober. Like some sci-fi transportation booth, the shower always offered an exit. He tilted back his head and let the hard, hot rays of water beam him up, or down, or anywhere. He turned Lisa's words in his mind, mouthed them with silent lips, as if washing them, also. Was she right? How many selves were jammed inside his head? The season of Beppe's first stroke came back to him. The old man — Club Trainer at the time — had been scampering across the field towards some injured player with his bucket and magic sponge when he had been struck down himself, literally *thrown* to the ground. He had lost the power of speech for some weeks afterwards. Mack was fifteen, playing his first season in the Senior side. Aldo, or Vince, or various Beppe-cousins or Beppe-nephews would wheel the stricken patriarch out to the sideline each Saturday thereafter — ostensibly to watch, but in fact to sleep. He had often seemed to Mack a kind of Club mascot, or big soft toy: small and aged and bent and stuffed with that thick tufty hair which poked untrimmed from various orifices. Now he seemed little more than a scarecrow, slumped in a wheelchair, his useless right arm pinned by its cuff to the front of his shirt.

A month passed, and the old man, still immobile, was speaking Italian as fluently as ever. But English —

his second language, his second self — never came back to him, as if the words were stored in different parts of his brain, behind different bulkheads. With the loss of language came a loss of memories, and a loss of love: the Beppe who survived felt no attachment to Mack, a stranger to his older, different self. It took many months of hurt and anger before Mack could accept this. At first, after the initial grief, he had hated the old man — or the impostor inside that jerky, marionette body.

A strange thing: Beppe looked older, but had grown younger, in a way. Years had been stripped from his mind, from his memory, if not from his body. He had somehow travelled backwards in time.

Mack shut off the water, stepped out and wrapped himself in a towel. As always in his arguments with Lisa — with anyone — the best answers came to him later. We're all like that, he should have told her: different selves for different times and places. Paul, Mack, Sweetheart — not to mention the self that spoke in tongues, under anaesthetic.

She was asleep, or feigning. No pink lamp tonight. Showered and dried, he crept in beside her, naked. He was tired, and still giddy with drink. He dozed and jerked awake, and dozed and jerked awake, finding himself, finally, trapped in some half-delirious, half-insensible mid-state. His thoughts, the actual focal point of conscious attention, seemed controlled more by random dice-spin than by force of will: a collage of memories and notions jostled through his brain without pattern.

'Do I ever talk in my sleep?' he asked over breakfast, again.

'You sound guilty.'

Her mood had lifted, as always — a self-defined Morning Person, all-forgiving when the sun was shining and her smile with it.

Mack was feeling less serene. His head ached, his thoughts, so active in the sleepless small hours, felt as sluggish as the thick honey he dripped across his cereal.

'No — I'm serious. Have you ever heard anything?'

'Have you something you want to confess?'

'That's the point. Maybe I have — I just wish I knew what it was.'

She laughed, and reached across her breakfast to squeeze his hand.

'You could sing the Hallelujah Chorus in your sleep and *I* wouldn't hear it.'

He spent the day in front of the television. Food helped fill the hours, and, after lunch, a little hair of the dog. Perhaps it was the alcohol that gave him the patience to watch cricket. More test pattern than Test match, he had always thought it: fixed, and unchanging. The game still bored him, yes — but it was a ritual, structured boredom. A boredom with limits. Or perhaps more a continual deferral of boredom, like travel. The contests passed with painful slowness, but they passed, measurably. The passage of time could be quantified: in run-rates, over-rates, drinks breaks, lunch, tea, stumps. And in commercial breaks: identical plugs for identical beers or identical cars, as repetitive as the ticks of a clock.

'You going to watch TV all day?'

'It passes the time.'

'You're welcome to come to the beach with me and Anthea.'

'Anthea's going to the beach?'

'What do you mean?'

'Doesn't seem like her scene. Too sporty. Too … outdoors.'

Her smile encouraged him to push further.

'Heaven forbid someone might mistake her for a jock.'

'You could at least try to like her, Paul. She likes you.'

He laughed, loudly, genuinely amused. 'She loathes me. She's jealous of me.'

'What do you mean?'

'What do you think I mean? Are you blind? She's always chipping away at us. At me. She even *sits* between us.'

She turned her face away, briefly. Perhaps there were tears in her eyes, but he didn't think so. When she faced him again, she was composed, and patient.

'I'll blame that on your blood alcohol.'

'Don't blame it — thank it.'

But he regretted speaking his mind, if not thinking his mind, the moment she had left. By the time she returned, late, from the beach, he had regretted the thought also, and apologised.

'The problem with sitting around all day,' he said, 'too much time to think.'

'Then come to the beach tomorrow.'

'Next week. I promise. When the splint comes off.'

But the removal of the splint did little to improve his mobility. At the end of January, still not fully weight-bearing, he decided to defer the milk round until second term.

'I'll believe it when I see it,' was Lisa's comment.

Her continuing scepticism irritated him, her refusal to take his career change seriously.

'I mean it. As soon as the knee's ready.'

'Whatever you say, sweetheart.'

11

'Good morning, Mr McNeil.'

The voice was Iain's, a sing-song classroom parody from the far side of the staff room. The first day of first term; he was sitting in his usual corner, an avuncular tom cat in a bow tie, greeting his staff as they arrived. His coffee mug sat on the table before him, PARTY ANIMAL emblazoned in bold letters on the side.

'If you insist,' Mack said.

'Ready for the fray?'

'As ready as I'll ever be.'

No autocrat, Iain spent more time in the staff room than in his office, one of the team, still 'working the chalk face'. He wanted to be loved, not obeyed, which meant his staff got away with murder.

'How's the trick knee?'

'Getting there.'

Mack took his own mug from its hook behind the urn: a gift, like many of the staff mugs, from Iain: YOU'D DRINK TOO IF YOU HAD MY JOB. He squeezed some half-hot water from the urn, mixed in a heaped spoonful of coffee, and headed for a different corner of the big room, unwilling to exchange further inanities. There was no escape; Iain rose and followed him across.

'A word in your shell-like?'

'Fire away.'

'I have some good news and some bad news.'

Another familiar phrase, if carrying more meaning: Iain's standard sugar-coating for bitter pills.

'Perhaps we'd better talk in the office.'

The office — never 'my' office — meant very bad news. Mack rose and silently followed his friend out one door and in through another. The Head's office, rarely used, was exemplary in its minimalism: grey metal filing cabinets, functional furniture, cream venetian blind in a curtainless window. Only the walls had been personalised, with an assortment of framed mottoes and exhortations. THINK! and YOU DON'T HAVE TO BE CRAZY TO WORK HERE BUT IT HELPS.

Iain perched himself, informally, on a corner of desk, unable to bring himself to sit behind it.

'Which do you want first?'

Mack eyed him, world-wearily, refusing to play the game. His friend shrugged.

'First the good news. I thought you might like to coach the tennis this term. Until you … leave.'

'In school hours?'

Iain nodded. 'Wednesday afternoons.'

This was fine with Mack, happy to coach marbles if it kept him out of a classroom.

'Pencil you in?'

'Ink me in. And the real news?'

Iain shifted, uncomfortably, and fiddled with his bow tie. 'If it was up to me, Mack. But it's Head Office. Out of my hands.'

'What is?'

The Head rose and stepped behind the big desk for the first time, more in search of protection than authority. He had enormous trouble with the role of Headmaster, laying down the law. A badge of office might help, Mack thought — an official robe to hide behind. An academic mortar-board, perhaps, donned like the black cloth cap of a judge sentencing prisoners to death, shifting the responsibility from the personal to the general, from the agent to the Law.

'Spit it out,' Mack prompted. 'You'll feel much better.'

Iain's eyes found his again, grateful even for ironic forgiveness, in advance.

'If you leave, Mack — you have to resign. No deferments. No leave without pay. There's a lot of pressure for permanent positions.'

'Is that all?'

'It means you can't come back,' Iain said.

He scrutinised Mack, then repeated his message, the

terrible burden of which did not seem to be getting through.

'If it doesn't work out — you can't come back.'

Mack beamed, then reached across the wide desk and pumped his friend's hand.

'Thank you. I don't know how you did it, but I knew you wouldn't let me down.'

Another joke, of course, but as the bell rang for first lesson, and he rose and left a mystified Iain standing in his wake, he couldn't see much badness in the news. Apart from having to pass the headlines on to Lisa. That might prove tricky; time and place would need careful thought. And a little judicious sub-editing. But the attraction of burning his bridges behind him grew with every step he took towards Year Five maths, and the race of little people he couldn't tell apart.

Pre-season

1

Mack had never forgotten the feel of Saturday mornings as a boy, of rising in the winter dark brimming with joy — a joy whose purity he recognised only now, as an adult, when he had the words to describe it.

He would silently lace up his boots at first light, and step softly about the kitchen with a bottle of milk or a big, weightless box of cornflakes, trying not to leave a telltale spoor of sprig-prints in the soft linoleum. But in the end not too worried, already far from kitchen and breakfast and a sleeping father.

Lisa had never understood this part of him. Amused at first, of late she was merely baffled.

'It was all I cared about,' he tried to explain, again, cleaning his boots before heading down to the Club. The splint was off, the knee, liberated, had been cleared by the surgeon. Pre-season waited.

'Fine, Mack. *Then*. But we're talking about now. You're a grown man.'

He levered a small wedge of hardened clay from between the sprigs, keeping silent. Perhaps he was far from her, also, time-travelling of sorts, at least emotionally. Lost once again in childhood, slipping eagerly from the house on Saturday mornings with a tightly pumped ball and an even more tightly inflated heart.

He had always been first at the Club, arriving even before the marking-out of the pitch, or the stringing of the nets. The pitch was a street's width from home — spitting distance, his father joked — but he would wait for hours outside the locked rooms. There were things to do, further preparations: banging his worn, flapping ball endlessly against the wall, volley, half-volley, left foot, right.

Often it must have been raining, the pitch a bog for much of the season, but he remembered none of that. From all the winters of childhood he could recall only the bracing freshness of the air, the perpetual cold, clear, holiday-blue of Saturdays.

The ritual preparations of those weekends had stayed with him, deeply etched: the Friday night boot cleaning, the Saturday morning packing of the bag, pads, socks, shorts and towel, always in strict order. These routines had the dimensions of a religious ceremony. Their incense was the powerful smell of boot polish and liniment. As an adult, such rites served more as a way of focusing concentration than as a way of keeping faith with the world, or influencing that world, but as a kid he had been paralysed by superstitions.

Beppe hadn't helped. Bent over his lime-spreader, he would follow the same inefficient routine every Saturday as he lined the grass. He might have been marking out some complex geometrical figure, according to fixed rules. First the left sideline, then the right. Far square, then near. Back to the centre circle, followed, in strict sequence, by the two opposite touchlines. He left till last the satisfying dab of the two penalty spots: two sharp full stops.

The first time Mack tried to help — ten years old, but even then unable to stand still and watch, wanting to be on the move, to be physically occupied — the old man had angrily snatched back the spreader.

'I only wanted to save time!'

'Brings bad luck,' Beppe muttered, and crossed himself, and with his boot attempted to erase the few feet of white lime that he would replace later in the sequence.

'Today you watch. Maybe the next week, help.'

Mack helped, more carefully, and soon learnt to share the old man's satisfactions. Each Saturday the lime flowed as evenly as milk onto the ground. The wheelbarrow waited at fixed rendezvous points ahead, the smooth white line unravelled behind. Slowly and painstakingly the boy and the man — roughly the same height, but with a lifetime of years between them — ruled their geometry across the green page of grass.

Afterwards Beppe would clamber to the top plank of the small wooden stand, roll a cigarette, and sit contentedly on the bench to survey his work: an exercise in symmetry.

'*Ho finito.* Now *you* must do the work.'

Symmetries were to be found everywhere, the boy soon discovered. When his own team won, he would recall everything he had done that morning before the game — every move, every task, every gesture — and attempt to repeat the lucky sequence of events the following Saturday: rising at the same time, pulling on his clothes in the same order, knotting his boots left to right, or right to left …

Even at fifteen, a teenage prodigy on the eve of his first training night with the senior squad, he had been consumed by fresh superstitions — eating no meat, walking backwards through his bedroom door, carrying his training bag in his left hand.

He had been first to arrive at the Club for that session, by some hours, sprinting home from school to prepare. Afterwards, physically exhausted, but high on his own adrenalin, he had not wanted to leave, ever. Even when Beppe sent him packing — 'homework hour' — he had taken an age to cross the narrow street. The night was dark, the air warm, the blueish flicker of televisions seemed aimed at him through open doors and windows all along the street. It was a world more heard than seen: television voices, the shoosh and chatter of the big water sprinklers out on the pitch, the low, throbbing warble of the cooped pigeons. The smell of the sprinklers saturated the air: a dark, moist perfume. Half-way between Club and home, stranded in the middle of the road, Mack halted. His bare feet were pressed against the still-warm bitumen, his boots were slung around his neck. He felt as happy as he'd ever felt in his life.

He had one ambition only: to do tomorrow exactly as he had done today.

Even now, near the end — after the injuries and operations, the wrecked knee, the endless grind of training, the Club intrigues — the feeling of those formative Saturdays and Tuesdays and Thursdays remained, unspoilt. To walk down through the wire cage of the players' race and out onto the smooth plane of green was still to forget all else. To play the beautiful game still left him somehow emptied, opened up, released; above all, somehow *clean*.

2

Pre-season is a trap. Younger players, keen to prove themselves, desperate to survive the first culling, sprint the warm-up jogs, push flat out through the sprints — and arrive the following week half-dead, their summer legs stiffened into hardboard. Old hands learn to pace themselves. First nights mean nothing, it's looking good in the coming weeks that counts.

All of which Mack knew, but he was unable to prevent himself arriving first at the Club, and being first out on the lush, spongy turf. Restless and fidgety, wanting a ball, he felt an urge to whistle, and see if one appeared.

Colby made him wonder why he'd been so eager. Summer was still on high-beam; the heat, exorbitant, daylight-saved, seemed to hoard its worst effects for the long evenings. The pale Anglos and freckled Celts in the team were soon beetroot-faced and glistening with sweat, but even the Italians were struggling. And still the sprints continued, end after end, hundred after hundred, till half the squad was bent double behind the northern goal, throwing up. Mack, some weeks behind the others in fitness, his knee still unresponsive, was worst affected. His legs turned to rubber, his wobbly muscles felt as if they had been somehow emptied of bulk, turned inside out.

In the background was a high, nagging voice. 'Anyone who doesn't want to be a winner, feel free to find another club.'

The coach stood on the touchline, a small man clutching a big clipboard and stopwatch, an array of coloured pens stuffed into his tracksuit pocket.

'Nowhere *near* the pace, Panozzo. I'll be taking a close look at your flowchart.'

'Flowchart?' Mack gasped. 'What the fuck is a flowchart?'

Bruno was also fighting for breath. 'Don't ask.'

'What is this? Soccer or athletics?'

'Pommy soccer. Kick and run. Kick the ball over the top and run 'em down. Four weeks and we haven't touched a fucking ball!'

Colby's voice carried from the far touchline. 'McNeil! If you've finished socialising, might we have the pleasure of your participation in the sprints? Too much to ask?'

'My knee's playing up,' Mack shouted back.

'Then what are you *doing* out here? I said I didn't want to see you till you were fit.'

'It's the other knee. The good knee. I felt something give. Maybe I'd better get some ice on it. Give it a rest.'

'Maybe you better give the bullshit a rest.'

'No,' Mack said. 'I'm getting Gino to look at it.'

He limped away in the direction of the Treatment Room, but Colby, unfinished, followed.

'I have a little rule you may not be familiar with, McNeil. Perhaps you'd like to hear it?'

'Not really. But I have a feeling I'm going to anyway.'

'No one leaves the field during training without my permission.'

The night was still; Colby's hard, yappy voice bounced against the stand. The other players stopped running, alert; a huddle of Members watched intently from the sidelines, *grappa* glasses frozen in their hands. Several more appeared in the doorway of the Club, clutching pool cues, Aldo among them.

Mack raised his arm as he continued walking away, his back to Colby. 'Please, Sir. May I have permission to leave the field?'

'You'd shoot yourself in the foot to get out of a day's work, McNeil.'

Aldo was waiting at the top of the race, eyebrow furrowed.

'Take it easy, Mack. What harm in asking if you can leave?'

'I *did* ask the little bastard if I could leave.'

Mack pushed past and clambered onto the bench in

the Treatment Room, a small, dark cave lined with shelves of bandages and bottles of liniment. Gino Trimboli, Club Trainer since the death of old Beppe, appeared in the door, incredulous.

'The *good* knee?'

Mack nodded.

'I don't believe it,' Gino said. 'Been doing your quads?'

'You name it, I've done it.'

Exercise was the only treatment Gino was conversant with, sometimes supplemented with a little ice. He squeezed a handful of muscle above the knee. 'Lost some bulk over summer. You sure you been doing them?'

'*Giuro sul segno della croce,*' Mack said, falsetto, crossing his heart. 'And hope to die.'

'You got to break these things in gently, Mack. You can't do too much on the first night.'

'Tell that to little Hitler.'

Gino refused to be drawn into Club politics.

'Ice-pack might be best,' he muttered, and fossicked in an antique yellow fridge, as disorganised as always.

The Trainer's job had been Beppe's for life — and now, it seemed, well into afterlife, for the Treatment Room was still *his* cave, hung with his ancient framed photographs, filled with his collection of Calabrian witch-potions and liniments that no one else was game to use. The same hot tang of menthol and camphor still filled the air, stinging the eyes, burning the throat like a shot of *grappa*. There was an antique pharmacy feel to the room: an apothecary's shop, its shelves lined with coloured glass vials and quaint jars. A new, gleaming ultrasound machine — a donation from the Club Social Committee — stood on a stainless steel trolley in a corner. No one had ever seen Gino, a bricklayer by trade, lay either of his big, blunt hands on it.

'Could try a little ultrasound,' he murmured, doubtfully.

'Ice will be fine.'

One of the younger players hopped through the door, clutching the back of his thigh.

'Calf?'

'Hamstring.'

Gino handed Mack a pack of frozen peas, and gestured to the door. 'Ten minutes on, ten off.'

The Club, smoke-filled, packed with sweating, arguing Members, had the stifling atmosphere of a sauna. Short, portly men with dark weatherbeaten faces were crammed about every table, drinking, shuffling cards, gesturing. This was their home away from home: *una seconda casa*, untroubled by the presence and demands of wives. Mack hobbled between the crowded tables, exchanging greetings, and escaped out into the open air. The Club had also been his second home, but his feelings tonight were more complex. He sat on the bottom plank of the stand, his knee extended horizontally, the pack of frozen peas moulded over it. Training was in full swing. Balls *had* appeared out on the pitch, of a kind. The players, seated on the grass in pairs, were tossing heavy medicine balls back and forth. Colby paced urgently between them, counting, loudly.

Aldo's voice came from somewhere behind Mack. 'Beer?'

'Ta.'

The beer was half-foam; tapping beer was not a skill the volunteer barmen — brandy drinkers, *grappa* drinkers — excelled at. Or perhaps half-full glasses were official Club policy: the profit margin was in the missing inch. He sipped, grateful at least for the coldness. The sunlight, even at eight, felt hot and heavy, unrefined, like a type of ore.

Aldo settled at his side nursing a Campari soda, topped with a slice of lemon, a drink that appeared far more expertly prepared. He set a small cardboard tube of *Baci* on the plank between them, another peace offering.

'How's the knee?'

'*Così, così.*'

'You gotta understand one thing, Mack. The coach has the committee's — and my — full support. Can't run the Club any other way.'

'Just keep him off my back till the knee comes good.'

Aldo changed subjects. 'How's the house?'

Or was it a more subtle way of discussing the same subject, a reminder of Mack's obligations?

'Laundry taps leak.'

'I'll send someone round.'

The two men sipped at their differently coloured drinks for a time, watching the players out on the flat grass. Bruno Panozzi, oldest by several years, was bent double again behind the goals, throwing up.

'We're looking to the future this year,' Aldo said. 'Bringing through the young talent.'

Bruno had lifted his big head and was looking their way, as though listening — although he was fifty yards away.

'It might be that some of the senior players have to take a pay cut. Chocolate?'

Mack shook his head. 'I like to earn them.'

Rebuked, Aldo picked an imaginary fleck of lint from his silk suit. His business might be failing, but he still looked the role. *Nascere con la camicia*, old Beppe would say. Born in a collared shirt. More northerner than southerner, a despised *polentone*, an eater of polenta.

'If it was just me, Mack, I wouldn't think of it. But some of the committee …'

Mack remoulded the pack of frozen peas, irritated.

Aldo consulted the committee on exactly nothing; these words were a favourite shelter.

'Don't see how *I* can take a cut. Ten percent of fuck-all is still fuck-all.'

Aldo laughed, nervously. 'Uh — there's the house.'

'What do you mean?'

The chairman paused before answering. 'Some of the committee thought … Maybe you could manage a token rent. A few dollars a week.'

Mack sipped his beer, declining to answer.

'You'd still be way out in front,' Aldo said, rising. 'Get you another beer?'

'You paying?'

Aldo grinned. 'Of course. Look — forget I said anything, Mack. It was just an idea someone tossed onto the table at committee. I'm on your side. I'll stop it going any further.'

Mack declined again to answer. Aldo shrugged, reclaimed the tube of chocolate kisses, and left him sitting there. The sun was finally setting, the flood lights, triggered by the failing light, began to glow, dull red at first, warming slowly to white incandescence, peering down onto the players like the multiple eyes of giant stick insects. Colour slowly faded from the sky and surrounding suburbs, but the pitch remained brilliantly lit: a forgotten piece of daylight left behind in the enclosing darkness. The field retained its vivid greenness among the surrounding black and grey shadows; the players in their bright strips might have been iridescent moths darting erratically about beneath the light.

Like moths they also seemed limited by some invisible border, zig-zagging back and forth as if rebounding from the walls of a glass cage.

Stranded on the sidelines, Mack felt a rush of nostalgia. Or self-pity, refracted into nostalgia. That oasis of colour and light had always moved him as a child. Flat on his stomach in his narrow bed, he would lift his head and watch through his bedroom window until the white heat of the lights faded, and the players pulled on thicker, longer clothes and retreated inside the Club rooms — little more than a tin shed in those early days. He could never sleep while things were happening across the road. On the warmer nights at each end of winter the Italians sometimes lounged outside the shed, or sat at card tables erected in smaller, portable cones of light, playing Broom and sipping their brandy or *grappa* from tiny, glinting glasses.

Much later would come the noise of voices leaving, bicycle bells tinkling, the occasional car or truck engine gunned into life: more engine noises and less bicycle bells as the years passed, and the immigrants prospered.

Gentle calls of *Ciao Beppe, Ciao Gino, Ciao, ragazzi!* and *Alla prossima settimana* echoed musically through the street, refrains that the boy always found soothing and reassuring as he lay in bed, a vaguely Latin benediction, or litany of chants and responses. *Buona notte.* Not even the music of the pigeons, warbling softly to each other in their loft at the side of the house, had the tranquillising power of this.

If he resisted sleep long enough, through heavy lids he would finally witness the ritual departure of old Beppe: carrying out the garbage, locking the Club room, then the change rooms, and finally padlocking the high wire gates of the ground itself, a strict ritual that never varied.

Beppe's last act of benediction, also, never varied. He always lifted a hand as he shuffled away up the street, as if in blessing, and threw a loud whisper towards the darkened window where the small boy from across the road was listening.

'*Sogni d'oro*, Paolo.' Dreams of gold.

Twenty years had passed since then but it seemed no more than twenty weeks. Mack rearranged the peas, thawing now, a bag of softening ball bearings. Where had the intervening years vanished? Surely it couldn't be over that quickly, a tiny township driven through at speed. Blink, and you miss it. The thought was too disturbing; he rose and hopped towards the exit, restless despite his exhaustion, wanting urgently to be elsewhere.

3

The knee stayed swollen. Mack skipped Thursday night training, and the Sunday morning beach and sandhill session. For the first time in his life he felt no disappointment; Colby and summer were a tag-team he was only too happy to avoid.

Summer continued to reschedule itself from January into February, February into March, the temperature climbing a little higher each day, dropping back a little less each night. No relief in sight, cool women announced after the news each night.

He was tempted to skip the Tuesday session as well. Lisa collected him after school and they washed away the day's heat and surface grime in the sea at Semaphore. But the knee felt good, perhaps the swimming helped; at home he showered and pulled on his training gear, if only to escape the hoarded heat of the house.

'You're not serious, Mack.'

'Gino can strap it up. I'll see how it goes.'

It went badly, giving way in the first ten minutes. Permission to leave the field was applied for, through the proper channel. Colby waved him off, amicably enough, and even sought him out in the Treatment Room a few minutes later.

'Doesn't look good?'

'It'll be fine.'

The coach paused, then asked, 'How many games you miss last year, Mack?'

'A couple.'

A moment of silent eye contact. Mack realised that Colby knew *exactly* how many.

The coach turned to the trainer. 'What do you think, Gino?'

'Coupla weeks — if he does his exercises.'

Mack found himself in the stand again a few minutes later, the inevitable pack of frozen peas — the same pack, refrozen — moulded about the knee. This week it was Vince Rossi who fetched out a cold beer, and one for himself, although the conversation, after a weather summary, followed much the same script as the last. How's The Knee? How's The House? — this beginning to sound like some sort of regular Reminder Notice. Vince's tone, though, was different: a note of genuine concern.

'Got your tickets for next week, Mack?'

'What tickets?'

'For the fundraiser.'

'I'm not much interested in fundraisers.'

'You'll be interested in this one.'

Mack was listening with one ear only, more interested in watching the training. A ball — a real ball, filled with weightless air not heavy medicine beans — had materialised on the grass; the sweating players were gathered about it, bemused, as if some giant mushroom or rare puffball had sprung from the watered turf overnight. Coloured bibs were handed about by Colby, and suddenly the players were into the final session, a sharp one-touch game, squeezed into half a pitch. Dangerous times always, often more dangerous than the real thing on Saturdays. Each player was intent on impressing the coach; one or two were happy to damage a team mate's ankles, or not *un*happy, if it meant forcing their own way into the opening line-up. Behind the goal, a few kids waited for the privilege of fetching any ball kicked out of play; Mack noticed the skinny boy among them.

'The Gentlemen's Evening,' Vince said somewhere.

For the first time he had Mack's attention. 'The what?'

'Colby's idea. Worked well at his last club, he says. A porn-and-prawn night.'

'Videos?'

'Live strippers.' Vince pulled a rubber-banded sheaf of tickets from his pocket. 'How many shall I put you down for?'

'Jesus, Vince — Beppe would turn in his grave.'

'I won't tell him if you don't. How many?'

'I dunno …'

'Come on, Mack. You've got to support these things.'

'One. Maybe.'

Ten tickets were peeled off and handed over. 'Flog all you can. I need the money by Sunday.'

Out on the turf, one of the new, younger players had taken a bag of balls to the far end of the ground and begun rehearsing free kicks: Mack's specialty. His own foot kicked slightly, involuntarily, each time the kid — tattooed, shaven-headed — struck the ball, in a reflex twitch, a kind of muscle-memory. As the ball spun into the corner of the net, he felt a vicarious pleasure: the sweet satisfaction of striking leather against its grain, spinning it like a top just *so*, and closing the eyes and knowing from that single touch precisely where the ball is heading.

'Remember Beppe's tinkling ball?'

Vince laughed. 'Dad had some crazy ideas.'

'It was a great idea. I loved it.'

'Mack, it's a wonder we didn't break our fucking legs. Running around the field blindfolded.'

The kid with the shaven head might have been wearing his own blindfold, and each of the balls in his bag might have enclosed its own jingling bell. He took another from the big string bag and set it on the turf. Three steps, a smooth left-footed caress, the ball dipping and swerving twenty yards into the top corner of the net.

And again, same spot exactly. And again.

Mack was reminded of another Beppe trick: suspending a toy balloon from the cross-bar at some chosen spot, risking his old bones on the summit of a step-ladder to tie the string. The first time Mack managed to burst the balloon brought a reward: his first chocolate kiss. He still remembered the motto: *Love is like the moon; if it does not grow bigger, it will grow smaller.*

'Looks like you've got some competition,' Vince said, somewhere in the present.

Mack agreed. 'Nice left foot.'

'That's young Watson. Came over with Colby. Package deal.'

'A skinhead.'

'They're all thugs out north. *Gli skins inglesi!*'

They laughed together, remembering the phrase, a favourite of Beppe's. The skinhead — the *skin* — aware he was being watched, spat nonchalantly onto the turf as he strutted back to take another kick.

'Looks like a bad case of fig jam,' Mack said.

'I'm not with you.'

'Fuck I'm Good, Just Ask Me.'

Vince laughed, obligingly. Out on the grass Colby

110

had gathered the players, and was strutting among them.

'McNeil!' he called up into the stand. 'Feel free to join us. Think your knee can stand a team talk?'

'You got problems there, mate,' Vince murmured.

'Is that some of the committee speaking, or is that you, Vince?'

'That's no one,' Vince said, and glanced about him, with mock terror. 'Did anyone say anything?'

His quiet laughter followed Mack down the steps and out onto the grass.

'Nice left foot,' he praised the skinhead, Watson, as they approached the huddle together.

The kid shrugged tersely, barely acknowledging the compliment, sure of himself, sated by too much praise — or not giving a stuff. He was wearing a crimson Arsenal training top. A biceps tattoo peeped from the sleeve: a Union Jack. *Uno skin*, for sure.

'Maybe I could show you a few tricks,' Mack offered, limping after him, but the kid walked on, still not bothering to answer.

'Just ask me,' Mack called, and laughed to himself, falling further behind.

4

Something was burning in the hills above Wog Heights. A thick column of smoke could be seen rising and expanding from behind the furthest ridge as Mack drove home from training. He had blamed the stuffy, cooked meat smell on the nearby abattoirs as he left the Club. Now he recognised it for what it was: roast mutton, carried on the dog breath of a hot north-easterly.

Somewhere up there a flock was burning.

The front door of the Display Home was open, bushfire bulletins blaring at full volume from both radio and television. Several cartons sat on the table, packed loosely with valuables: wedding photography, best silver, assorted ornaments. Soccer trophies. He found Lisa in the bedroom, pulling clothes from her wardrobe.

'Just in case, Mack.'

'It's serious?'

The house was still glowing with the day's compacted heat. Lisa, stripped to black underclothes, shone with sweat. Mack jerked open the French doors and stepped out onto the verandah; she followed. The stink of cooked mutton was thicker now, and more oppressive. No naked flames could be seen, but the belly of the cloud of smoke looming above the next valley was a violent, flickering red, a dark screen onto which images from the inferno beneath were projected.

'Where is it?'

'Basket Range. Moving away. No real problem unless the wind shifts. But we should take some precautions.'

'I'll fill the gutters — just in case. And a few buckets inside the house. I should have cut the grass.'

'I've been asking you for weeks,' she reminded him, but gently.

The wooden frames of the failing housing development surrounded them, less timber now than tinder. They stood together on the verandah, aware of their isolation.

'Maybe Aldo started the fire,' Mack said, trying to lighten the mood.

Lisa laughed. 'Aldo would have been more careful. He would have made sure the wind was blowing *this* way.'

They spent the evening moving through the house, packing irreplaceables, finishing in the bedroom sorting favourite clothes. By nine the fire had been 'contained' but they continued packing, beginning to enjoy the drama, wanting to prolong its spicy possibilities, even half-hoping that the wind would change, and the front turn back towards them.

'You can't be too careful,' Lisa said, in the parody voice she sometimes adopted, half her mother-in-law, half her own mother.

As they packed their suitcases, sweating, in the hot, enclosed bedroom, it felt as if the house *was* burning. From time to time their bodies brushed together; at first accidentally, then more deliberately and knowingly. Nothing needed to be said, neither thermometer reading nor pink scarf was required as Mack lifted the suitcases off the bed.

There was no real danger, but to make love in the heat while the hills burnt close behind them seemed suddenly, recklessly thrilling. Mack was painfully stiff inside his shorts; Lisa's gaze had become hard and fixed. They climbed onto the bed from opposite sides, simultaneously.

She found the tickets for the Gentlemen's Evening the next morning, in a tracksuit pocket where he'd left them.

'*Entertainment For Men?*' she read.

'Christ! I'd forgotten! When is it?'

'More to the point, *what* is it?'

'Club Fundraiser. A porn-and-prawn night.'

She laughed, dismissively, and tossed the tickets aside. 'How sordid. Do they really think anyone will go?'

Mack hesitated. 'It's semi-compulsory. The Club expects the senior players to support these things.'

'You're not serious?' She asked, then paused, and

laughed again, incredulous. 'You're teasing me.'

'It might be fun,' he said. 'Why don't we make up a table? Anthea would *love* to come.'

Risky words, teetering on the edge of the unforgivable. Lisa's packed suitcase was still sitting on the bedroom floor, as if in some midday television drama; she could easily have taken offence, reached down, picked up that suitcase and walked out.

'Why do you say things like that, Mack? It's not funny. It's just … crude.'

Her rebuke came with a shake of the head more bemused than angry; it came from the head, not from the heart. The glow of last night's love-making was still strong in the small, hot room, and the night they had spent in bed, close together despite the heat. The loose cannon of his tongue had been forgiven, again.

Her disapproval of the Gentlemen's Evening was disguised till the last minute in a jokey disbelief that he *would* actually attend.

'You'll need a pair of brothel creepers. You wouldn't want to be under-dressed.'

She continued to think — or feigned to think — that Mack was teasing until the moment he walked out the door the following Friday night.

'I can't believe you would do this!' she called after him, still more puzzled than angry. 'I can't believe you would do anything so sleazy!'

Her words seemed to follow him down the steps and into the car, staying with him, as if she was sitting in the passenger's seat. He slipped the gearshift into neutral and rolled down the drive, out onto the slope of the street. Given luck with the traffic lights, it was possible, theoretically, to coast all the way across the city to Regal Park.

He had never quite achieved the feat, but continued to make the effort, if only to distract himself.

5

'You're drooling, Bruno.'

The big man was wedged behind a corner table at the Club, eyes fixed on the plumpish, topless waitress behind the bar. The usual misshapen cigarette smouldered between his fingers. Mack set a jug of beer and clutch of frosted glasses on the table and joined him.

'Nothing to get excited about,' he said.

'Looks fine to me,' Bruno said. 'Looks fucking *great*.'

'Down, boy. Keep yourself tidy.'

Despite Mack's feigned nonchalance — Been-There-Done-That — he felt an instant sweet release as he walked through the door. The day's tensions drained from him as if exhaled like smoke, smoothly and evenly, and with them all memory of Lisa's parting words.

He felt, simply, at home. Not even Colby could take that from him.

His home was crowded. A clock-steady disco beat pounded from somewhere up front: a beat so deep, or poorly amplified, that it was felt rather than heard above the roar of bar conversations: a rhythmic, seismic shaking of the floor and furniture. Three women in bikini bottoms and wet T-shirts were prancing among the tables, pressing soft upper body parts against the Gentlemen, slipping the heads of the most favoured inside their stretched T-shirts, between breasts, or planting themselves astride laps, fleetingly and teasingly, legs spreadeagled.

'The redhead's not bad.'

'Seven out of ten,' Bruno determined.

'And the degree of difficulty factor?'

Bruno laughed. A queue had formed of younger players, each clutching a wad of money, each waiting to remove the clinging T-shirt from the redhead with their teeth. Twenty dollars a bite. The skin — Watson — was among them, not yet eighteen, Mack guessed, too young to legally drink the beer he was spilling down his checked flannel shirt. A pair of dark glasses were wrapped around his shaven head, a stupid waste, or diminishment, of the view.

Mack turned his attention back to the stripper. Her smile seemed absurdly warm amid these sharks in feeding frenzy, but perhaps she was safe enough. Two thick-necked bouncers stood nearby; an older woman — fully clothed in a business suit, impeccably groomed — watched primly from a corner.

Vince Rossi, sitting ringside at the committee table, turned and shouted, a twenty-dollar note folded neatly between his fingers. 'I'll shout you, Macca. You look like you want to get your teeth into it.'

'Haven't had my rabies shots,' Mack shouted back.

Bruno urged him on. 'Bullshit, Mack. Get out there. You can't wait.'

Colby, on his way back to the committee table with a jug of beer, winked at Bruno as he passed. '*Bella*, eh son?'

His pretension irritated Mack less than his familiarity. This is not *your* home, he wanted to tell the coach.

'*Penultima sillaba,*' he shouted instead.

'Eh?'

'The stress is on the second to last syllable.'

The coach shrugged and pushed on, unfazed, willing for once to be corrected.

'Pretentious arsehole,' Mack muttered. 'Three months to learn one fucking word.'

Bruno laughed. 'Hey — look in the mirror sometime!'

The madam in the power-suit clapped her hands and her girls pranced off into the change rooms; Mack's teeth were spared the clinging T-shirt. The entrance to the inner sanctum was blocked by bouncers, casually but unmistakably. The bar re-opened. Money, after all, was the true purpose of the Evening: fundraising. Two topless, dumpling-breasted barmaids appeared behind the taps; the clamour of music and shouting and whistling was replaced by the deafening roar of a hundred bar-conversations.

'Whose shout?'

'Must be mine.'

Bruno rose, and waded into the press of bodies. Vince, sitting at the committee table, brought over his empty glass to join Mack. His shoes tonight were plain brown, Mack saw, mildly amused.

'Didn't bring the missus then?' Vince said.

Mack grinned. 'I'm surprised yours let *you* come.'

'She couldn't get me out of the house quick enough.'

'Makes sense. You get your fill here, you'll leave her alone.'

Their heads were close together, almost touching; there was no other way of communicating.

Vince said, 'So what's your excuse? You getting knocked back too?'

'Happens all the time these days.'

'I thought they only went off it after the kids arrived.'

'It's all science in our house. I only get to touch her when her temperature's up.'

He regretted his words as soon as he uttered them, a small betrayal of Lisa. But perhaps on a night of naked flesh, the naked truth was small beer.

Vince laughed again. 'Roll on, the flu season. But I think you got it wrong, mate. You do it when the thermometer's *down*. That's the safe time of the month.'

'Depends if you want to have them, or prevent them.'

'You want to *have* them? Mate — all you have to do is ask! You can have one of ours. You can have *two* of ours!'

Bruno worked his way back through the crowd with a foaming amber jug held high above his head, precariously sloshing.

'Working tonight?' Vince asked.

The big man nodded. 'Should be sleeping,' he shouted. 'The depot opens at midnight. But I couldn't miss this.'

The music started again: heart-pounding, its pulse rate much faster than the low, even heart-beats of the gathered athletes, but soon, perhaps, lifting theirs to its more excited, exalted state. The moment had been carefully judged, a certain restlessness had begun to ripple through the packed room, a feeling of expectation, of suspense.

Half a dozen tables had been pushed together during the break: a long, makeshift catwalk now ran down the middle of the room.

'Let's have a big hand for Monique,' a blurred, over-amplified voice announced.

A blonde woman, wearing bulky army fatigues, climbed deftly onto the tables and began marching up and down, mock-military style. At each end she saluted, high-kicked, and about-faced, smartly.

'Have a look at Colby,' Vince shouted in Mack's ear. 'He's almost blowing.'

Mack was more interested in Monique. Her military top was suddenly off — a movement so fluid, so simple, that he couldn't understand how she had done it — and the press of men was cheering and shouting, pushing forward, a school of reef fish turning, instantly, together. Of course most of the gathered assembly *were* Gentlemen, of a kind, taken singly. But here, together, they formed a new, composite creature: the mob, the gang, the herd. The team.

Those at the back, Mack among them, were forced to clamber onto their own tables to get any kind of view. Straightening, he glimpsed himself in the bar mirror beyond the stripper, standing on a table top, staring. What *was* he doing? Monique couldn't hold a candle to Lisa, who stripped for him nightly, privately. The stripper's body was youthful — soft and smooth-skinned, the baby-pink nipples possessing a swollen teenage tenderness — but the face above seemed to be some years, or even decades, older.

It was a face that had been places, known things; a hard, tough face.

Her last piece of clothing, a G-string, was kicked off. Her pubic delta was unshaven: a pinkness opened slightly within the furry gash as she high-kicked, this side, that side, to the beat of the roaring, clapping Gentlemen. She had been dancing for some minutes; her smooth body glistened. The sweat, and the unshaven delta: these were the human touches, the imperfections that brought her high gloss, magazine perfection to life. Despite himself, and the sight of himself in the bar-mirror that had briefly shamed him, Mack was aroused for the first time that night. Bruno, up on the table beside him, a hippo on tiptoes, had moved beyond arousal into the realm of pain.

'Jesus Christ!' he groaned. 'Jesus Christ!'

The music stopped, Monique's legs slid slowly apart, her body slipped slowly downwards, a perfectly executed splits, naked, on the table top. Then she rolled off and was gone.

The music stopped, the same blurred, amplified voice jarred the silence: 'Bar's open, gentlemen.'

The spell — hormonal, sexual — was broken, the fish school scattered. Conversations resumed, reluctantly; men climbed down from their table tops, or moved back to their seats, individuals again, more or less.

Vince shouted, 'She must be fit.'

'Fitter than you, maybe.'

He laughed. 'Better get her out to training.'

123

'At least you'd get a full turn-out.'

Bruno, suddenly sleepy, was staring into his beer. 'What do you think they get paid?'

'Is *that* what interests you?'

The big man smiled slowly, defensively. 'Just wondered.'

'A thousand,' Vince said.

'Each?'

He laughed. 'The whole circus.'

Mack slipped into arithmetic teacher mode. 'There must be, what, five girls? Plus bouncers. Barmaids. And the madam's going to take a bit. What do you think, seventy each?'

'It's cash,' Vince reminded him. 'Money under the table.'

'Nice work if you can get it,' Bruno murmured.

'You reckon?' Mack said. 'Seventy bucks for *that*? In front of ... these?'

'They probably do three shows a night,' Bruno said.

'Let's find out,' Vince said, and rose and headed towards the change rooms.

The shark pack was reassembling for the next feeding. A different stripper would perform, the MC promised, 'acts of real simulated sex' with a 'volunteer' from the committee table. Despite this news, Bruno's eyes had closed, his head was sinking towards the table, a faint, rhythmic snore escaped from his open mouth.

Mack detached the sagging toke from his fingers, took two long drags, snuffed out the butt with tweezered fingertips, and replaced it in Bruno's unmoving hand. Vince returned, skirting the crowd, with Monique in tow, fully clothed in military khaki. The attention of the crowd was focused elsewhere, no one noticed as she slipped into the empty chair between Mack and Bruno.

Vince, still standing, bent and shouted in her ear. 'What's your poison?'

'Southern Comfort,' she shouted back; he headed towards the empty bar.

She gave Mack a polite smile, then turned away, watching the backs of the huddled crowd.

'Liked your dancing,' he said.

'What?'

'I liked your dancing!'

He lip-read the answer: 'Ta.'

'Hot work.'

'The lights are the worst.'

'Maybe you're running a temperature.'

Something in his tone turned her head towards him again, a quizzical look.

'Sorry,' he said. 'Private joke. You on again later?'

She shook her head. 'Another show. In the city.'

Her age was still indeterminate. Despite the thick cladding of cosmetics and the toughness of the face she couldn't have been much more than twenty. She was smiling, but her teeth — the ribs of that smile — were a little worn and uneven. Malnourishment? Drugs? Mack was having difficulty thinking in terms other than cliché. He was also having trouble maintaining his end of a conversation. Vince returned with fresh drinks, but even he was keeping his distance, a Gentleman again, his conversation a little hesitant and formal, even respectful — or as respectful as any conversation that was shouted could be. Later, this memory would amuse Mack: they were both less relaxed in her company, fully clothed, than when she had stood on the table tops, naked.

Monique, familiar with the problem, deftly assumed control.

'Looks like he's enjoying himself,' she shouted, indicating the sleeping Bruno.

'Starts work in a couple of hours,' Vince explained.

'What's he do?'

'Milkman.'

The word sounded funny, or vaguely bawdy; they all laughed, although none could have explained why.

A final chorused cheer signalled the end of the routine; the music ceased, the mob dispersed again to various tables. Monique, sitting beside Mack, wrapped in drab khaki, earnt barely a passing glance.

Vince shouted in her ear: 'If you've finished, do you have to hang around? I'm about to leave. I'll give you a lift home.'

She gave him her best come-on pout. 'No can do. We've got a midnight show in the city. I'll leave you my number.' She pressed a small gilt-edged card onto the table, and rose. 'Ring me another time. Thanks for the drink, guys.'

'That went well,' Mack laughed, as she walked away.

'All part of the tease,' Vince declared. 'Probably a fucking virgin. Probably a Sunday school teacher earning a bit of fucking pocket money on the side.'

He pocketed her business card all the same. The music stopped; the women and their protectors vanished. The night was over; a collective tristesse pervaded the Club, a feeling of anti-climax, although not necessarily a sexual anti-climax. It was more the feel of all Closing Times, a night of drinking and shouting coming to an end without proper, ceremonial finish; a petering out.

'Last drinks, gentlemen!'

But the Gentlemen were already evaporating into the night. Bruno's snore had gained intensity, foregrounded by the relative quiet. Vince glanced at Mack across the slowly heaving hump of their friend's back.

'What do we do with this sack of shit?'

'I'll take him to the depot,' Mack said. 'Load his truck for him.'

'What the hell — I'll come too. The night is young.'

127

'The night is little,' Mack corrected him, and both laughed at the joke, a Beppe mistranslation. *La notte è piccola* ...

'One for the road?' Vince said, and poured out the dregs of the jug.

They pulled Bruno to his feet, and half-pushed, half-supported him, stumbling, outside. Alcohol had loosened the big man's musculature into a softer substance, more difficult to manage.

'Keys,' Mack shouted in the nearest ear, and when Bruno failed to answer, pushed him face-down over the bonnet of his milk truck, and began to frisk him, police-movie fashion.

'Careful,' Vince said. 'Might find something down there you don't fucking expect.'

A jingling keyring was extracted with difficulty, and Bruno eased over the side and into the tray of his own truck, limp as a sack of cement.

They climbed into the cabin from opposite sides, Mack behind the wheel.

'You okay to drive?'

'Been worse. Where to?'

'Let's get some coffee into the Hulk first. Hindley Street?'

'Sounds good.'

'You need to ring Lisa?'

'She'll be asleep. Carla?'

'She'll be awake. But if I'm lucky she won't even notice I'm not there. It's like a zoo, mate. Kids and nappies and shit everywhere. Not to mention the mother-in-law. The full Mediterranean catastrophe.'

Caffeine raised Bruno magically from the dead: three short blacks fetched out from a café and poured down the funnel of his open mouth as he lay spraddled in the back of the utility truck. His normal half-mute torpor had been deepened into coma by the beer and cannabis; coffee provided a partial antidote. Resuscitated, propped between his friends inside the cabin of the truck, he began to recover the power of speech.

'Whassa time?'

'Midnight. Where to?'

'Mile End,' he mumbled. 'The depot. Jesus — I don't feel so good.'

'If you want to throw up,' Vince said. 'Just yell.'

'But not in technicolour,' Mack added.

The truck crossed the Hilton Bridge, doubled back beneath, and drove parallel to the railway yards for some distance.

'Here,' Bruno pointed, several moments too late.

Mack braked, and reversed up the road, then turned in, backing the truck into a loading bay. Big dented metal milk churns lined the waist-high dock; a stale dairy smell — sour, yoghurty — pervaded the place.

Men in rubber boots and yellow plastic trousers hosed spilt milk into the drains, or hauled the crates of litre-cartons out from the big cold rooms, piled four or five at a time on hand trolleys. A miscellany of vehicles awaited the morning's deliveries: utilities, vans, small trucks, and cars towing trailers. Mack and Vince quickly threw their share of crates into the tray of the truck, and Bruno roused himself to scrawl an illegible signature, or cross, on some sort of invoice.

As they drove away he seemed to be approaching full consciousness.

'Fellas, I really appreciate this. Fucking brilliant.'

'We'll send you our bill. Just tell us where to start.'

'Uh — the left turn back there.'

The destination was reached after further backtracking and detours. Mack began working one side of the first street, Vince the other; Bruno crawled the car jerkily from house to house, fumbling loose change out through the window when needed, directing his assistants to the more difficult drop-spots that were hidden behind pot-plants, or in dark corners. And warning them, if he remembered, against the bigger dogs.

The crates in the tray of the truck emptied slowly. A competition developed between the two men, pleasantly half-drunk themselves, south side of the street versus north, with the truck their fulcrum, a kind of equilibrium point. Vince soon fell several houses behind; Mack, younger and fitter, moved half-way up the street ahead, enjoying the rhythm of it all. His knee didn't seem to trouble him, and after the first few streets he found himself on auto-pilot. The processes of delivery and collection of loose change performed themselves to some extent. The scribbled notes, taped or weighted to a doorstep — NO MILK TODAY, EXTRA HALF LITRE PLEASE, NO DELIVERIES TILL FRIDAY — registered, and were obeyed, at some half-conscious level.

'Let's change sides,' he suggested as the two men coincided at the truck.

Vince was panting, out of breath. 'Fine by me.'

A few streets later Mack, always competitive, was back in front again; and a few streets after that Vince was inside the cabin, driving, and Bruno was out working the other side of the street. A few streets after *that* — it seemed no more than a few to Mack, although his watch now showed 5 a.m. — the crates were empty apart from a few spare or damaged cartons, and they were driving, with Bruno behind the wheel, back to the Club.

The stars were fast-fading above, the rim of hills to the east sharpening into a knife-edge against the pale sky behind. Lights were blinking on in bedrooms and kitchens as they drove, the odd car or pushbike was pulling out into the dark streets, heading off to early morning shifts.

'Thirsty work,' Vince said.

'You got a key to the bar?' Bruno asked.

Vince shook his head. 'Where can you get a drink at this hour?'

'Sportsman's Hotel,' Bruno told him, immediately. 'Open all night.'

'You a sport, Mack?'

'It might be nice to be there when Lisa wakes up.'

Vince pulled a small card — the stripper's gilt-edged card — from his shirt pocket, and waved it in Mack's face.

'The night is little with us,' he said, grinning.

The truck turned in at the Club carpark, and stopped. Mack climbed out with a fixed smile, weary now of his friends' company. As he unlocked his car, Vince's voice called from behind.

'Mack! Think quick!'

He turned to find a carton of milk flying through the air towards him; he caught it, fumbling, at the second grab.

'What's this for?'

'Your alibi.'

6

'You might have rung, Paul.'

The name, once rare, had become his again in recent weeks, returned to him, a rechristening.

'I didn't want to wake you.'

'What if I *was* awake? What if I woke in the middle of the night? I might have been sick with worry.'

'You never wake.'

Lisa rose into a sitting position, jerked the usual succession of tissues from a box at the side of the bed, and wedged them between her thighs. He had crept into the house to find her, in fact, awake, if only by minutes, her thermometer propped between her lips. She had carefully noted the reading before speaking; even then her first words had nothing to do with where he had spent the night. Her temperature was rising, his presence was required in bed — or the presence of parts of him, at least.

'We'll talk later,' she had said, peeling off her pyjama top. She had copulated with him — the mechanical word described the act perfectly — with her face averted, avoiding any sign or show of love, apart from what was, paradoxically, perhaps the *least* intimate aspect of their lovemaking: the bare necessities of the act itself. The hydraulics. Above all, she had not kissed him.

'You smell like a brewery,' she excused herself, but he realised, in the dump of sadness that followed the wave of pleasure, that she had not kissed him for some time; that even the usual farewell or welcoming cheek-peck had ceased, somewhere in the near past.

'*Did* you wake?'

'No — lucky for you.'

'Then what are we arguing about?'

'The principle.'

'Can we discuss this later? When I've had some sleep?'

'I want to discuss it now, Paul. You've been out all night. I think I deserve an apology.'

'Okay. I'm sorry. Bruno was off his face. Someone had to help out with his round.'

'Ever heard of a phone?'

'It was too late. I could have rung to see if you were awake. Then you *would* have been.'

The circularity of this gave her pause; their disagreement had come full circle also, advancing nowhere.

'So how was it?' she asked.

'Tacky — but fun. The kind of thing you should do once.'

'I don't mean that. I don't want to hear a word about *that*. How was the milk round?'

'The milk round was fun, too.'

'Then the career change is still on?'

'It's what I want.'

She slipped naked from the bed, entered the bathroom, and turned on the shower. Mack flopped back among the pillows, exhausted. His eyes closed, sleep was drowning him in its rising honey. The soothing rush of the water carried to him, and its various sub-harmonies, smooth and tuneless, as Lisa's body shifted beneath it. His last thought was a realisation. His overnight absence was a minor sin. But if the little wrinkled sack that hung between his legs — the Family Jewels, in Lisa's words — had been missing in the morning, there would have been hell to pay.

The realisation might have been either amusing or saddening, but arrived in his mind as a simple fact, unadorned by feeling, as if his weary emotions had already fallen asleep, preceding his conscious mind.

The Season

1

April brought the first match of the new season. The weather was cooler, marginally, but its shapes and colours gave no forecast of rain: enamel-blue skies, long, warm days marred only by the occasional haze of topsoil that blew in from the north and remained suspended above the city, becalmed — a reminder that beyond the manicured lawns and rose-beds, and the rich pasture of a thousand irrigated sporting surfaces, there was a world of summer drought and fire and crop failure.

Inside the city limits there was no shortage of water. To drive down to the Club each evening was to run a gauntlet between countless water sprinklers and their scattering arcs. Viewed from the balustrade at Wog Heights, the city might have been a single green expanse of lawn, one vast park, miles wide, dotted with trees and houses. Remove the fences that divided those houses, and Mack felt he could push a mower from the hills to the sea, without once leaving grass.

The indefinite postponement of winter had left the various playing fields unrutted and unmuddied. The

Club pitch itself, evenly rolled and watered, was as green and true as billiard felt.

For the first time in years Mack found himself starting from the bench. Or worse: spending the entire game stuck fast to the bench and not playing at all. Publicly he blamed the knee; privately, if not consciously, he was half-grateful for the excuse of injury, sensing that he'd be sitting on the bench, fully fit or not. Interrogated by Colby on the progress of The Knee, he hedged bets, leaving himself a way out, with honour, if he wasn't picked. *Not quite up to a full game. Might not last the distance.* To be dropped from the starting eleven, fully fit, was unthinkable. After Thursday training he allowed himself the excuse of a slight limp as Saturday's opening line-up was pinned to the noticeboard, with his name printed below the line, among the substitutes, not above.

A limp which vanished, or was forgotten, by the following morning.

Sitting in the dugout during those first games, it was tempting to slip into the role of Senior Player, a team elder statesman, semi-retired, his role mostly advisory, a resource of experience and expertise. For the first time ever, he became familiar with the customs of that strange transit zone, The Bench. Seating protocol in the squat low-roofed shelter was strict: Colby central, Gino Trimboli on his left with his bag of first-aid tools and bucket and magic sponge, the Reserves Coach on his right. Squeezed in on both sides were the substitutes — older players on the way out sitting next to teenage whiz kids on the way up — joking uneasily among each other, occasionally encouraging their team mates on the field, but more often subtly criticising them, finding fault with those they hoped to replace.

Often one player would be singled out, the substitutes left on the bench concentrating their attentions, working as a team, united in an attempt to undermine his position.

'Is Stav carrying an injury?'

'Something's wrong. He's not moving freely.'

'I reckon he's done an ankle.'

Colby ignored such games: his mind — and mouth — was on the larger game. His hard, high-pitched voice carried easily to the far side of the pitch.

'Zervos — lift, son! Get your bleedin' arse into gear! Work harder.

'Bruno! Bruno, look at me, fuck you! The little bastard — what is he, porcelain? Let him know you're there! Go *through* the little bastard, son!'

Now and again, from the side of his crooked mouth, he would advise Mack to warm-up, on the sidelines, in public, in front of the small stand. An ancient tactic, this, used as a threat to the players on the field. The sight of a substitute sprinting the sidelines — 'Out there, where they can *see* you' — stretching hamstrings or quads, peeling off a tracksuit top was usually enough to scare any slacker into lifting his game.

Then Mack, duty done, would be instructed to pull his tracksuit on and return to the bench.

'If you'd stayed out there another minute I would have given you best player,' Gino whispered in his ear after one such display.

Mack's answer was loud enough for Colby to hear: 'I did more than some of them.'

For once the coach seemed sympathetic. 'You got as many touches as those bleedin' girls playing up front,' he said, but chose to make no substitutions.

The warm days lasted into May, and still Mack found himself on the bench, watching, or limping out of the Club rooms after training. At home the terrace was still his preferred happy hour venue; daylight saving had ended, but the balmy evenings permitted a drink outside with Lisa after training if she was home or, more often, a contemplation of the sunset, alone, if she was not. These had an end of the world feel to them: multi-coloured incandescence, a slow, silent fireworks spectacular. Prosaic explanations were offered on the nightly weather forecast — volcanic ash in the upper atmosphere, an eruption half a world away — but Mack preferred his magic, unexplained.

Mid-May, Bruno followed him home after Thursday

training to discuss the milk round, although not so much with Mack as with Lisa. The three of them sat outside, sipping cold beer in the cooling evening, watching the fireworks.

'You drinking light beer, Mack?'

'Been hitting it a bit hard lately. I need a break.'

This was in part a sop to Lisa, a softening-up. Selling the milk round would need all the help and tact it could get.

'Going to Italy,' Bruno told her, after a little prodding from Mack. 'Coupla months. Try out with a coupla clubs. Need someone to mind the shop. Someone I know.'

'You don't think a friend is the worst person?' Lisa suggested. 'What if something goes wrong?'

Silence followed, an empty space in the conversation, framed inside the sound of the distant city traffic, and somehow emphasised by that frame. Mack was forced to ask questions he had hoped she would ask, ritual questions to which he already knew the answers.

'How long does the round take?'

'Four hours. Five. Bit longer at first.'

More silence. A single dog bark carried up from the suburbs below, sharp against the dull background of traffic. Bruno, half-mute at the best of times, was sprawled in a straining canvas chair, tilting beer into his wide, flat face. His body seemed at times too big for his mind: a brontosaurus body so large that nerve-impulses took a measurable time to travel from the brain to the distant muscles. And yet his ability to think on the field never failed to surprise. Unable to call on any reserves of speed, he relied instead on an infallible game-sense: a canny ball-reading or mind-reading that enabled him to be in the right place at the right time, always. His movements were lumbering, but he was never more than a yard behind his smaller, fleeter opponents when the ball arrived, and often a yard in front. More often still, and more painfully for them, Bruno would be neither behind nor ahead, but occupying exactly the same physical space.

'What time do you start?' Mack pressed on, still for Lisa's benefit.

'Pick up the milk anytime. Need to start later this weather.'

He didn't elaborate. Lisa opened her mouth, lured into asking. 'Why?'

'The heat. Can't leave the stuff out too long. Turns into yoghurt. On the other hand, leave it too late, the customers get twitchy.'

The sun and its fireworks had gone, but a few fine ribs of cloud, hot-pink in colour, remained high in the west, at the edge of the deep blue-black velvet of night. The tranquillity of the evening was proving contagious;

Lisa sounded almost relaxed as she asked the question that most concerned her.

'What will Mack be making out of it?'

'Everything. Minus a few overheads. Paperwork. Truck lease.'

'I've done the sums,' Mack said. 'Milk round plus match payments. It's about the same as my teaching salary.'

'What match payments?'

'Okay — the rent. It's the same as a payment.'

'You seem to have made up your mind already,' she said. 'I don't suppose anything I say will change it. If it's what you want, Mack — okay. As long as you can have your old job back. If it doesn't work out.'

Her tone was mild, the form of her words less severe than their content. The serenity of the sunset had done its work.

Mack said, 'I'll have that in writing.'

Bruno spoke his first words for some time. 'It's honest work, Lisa. Nothing wrong with it.'

'Of course. I'm sorry — I didn't mean … But you're not a married man. Mack has others to think of.'

She was dissembling, Mack saw — covering her tracks. But the phrase jarred, an odd choice. Who were those others? The children they could not have?

'Have you eaten, Bruno?' she asked, still trying to repair any hurt done to him. 'There's plenty of food.'

'Great.'

'You like pasta?' Mack said.

An old joke, still worth a laugh. Lisa rose, squeezed behind Mack's chair and vanished into the house to prepare the food. Bruno's big saurian head turned slowly, watching her.

'Classy lady.'

'Thanks,' Mack said, feeling the usual absurd pride in her grace, as if he could somehow share the credit.

'The house ain't so bad either. For a wog house.'

'The view's good.'

A pause, while Bruno turned his head back.

'So how's the knee coming?

'*Così, così.*'

Jesus — we need you out there, Mack! Some of these kids …'

'A couple of them can play.'

'Maybe. But they're so fucking quiet. We need your mouth out there.'

'Colby's got a mouth.'

'We need it on the field. Someone to run things. Talk it up. Get these kids to play *angry.*'

Mack almost laughed out loud. Bruno was the least angry player he knew, unhurried to the point of serenity.

'The team's doing all right.'

'Lucky, is the word. It ain't the same. It ain't soccer.'

The big man paused, groping for a better term. 'It ain't … pretty.'

He paused again, and blinked, as if surprised by the force of his own eloquence, or embarrassed to find himself flattering his team mate, however obliquely. His tone, when he resumed, was gruffer.

'You doing your exercises?'

What to answer? The longer Mack limped about, the more of a problem the knee became — in his head. He knew this only too well; he had seen it in other players. However complete the recovery, injury leaves a residue of caution. Physical innocence — the deep, subliminal sense of invulnerability, never articulated because never questioned — is lost, and with it the passion of play, the rapture which is born, in part, of carelessness.

'I do my quads every night.'

'You should swim. With flippers.'

'And floaties?'

Bruno laughed, but Mack found the discussion uncomfortable. The more he talked, or even joked, about his injury the worse it seemed to get. This, too, he had seen in others. The spreading ripple of a strained knee or groin or ankle, the way other parts of the body begin to need conserving and nursing. Until suddenly — waking in the morning stiff-jointed, or easing some aching body part into a deep, hot bath at night —

another threshold is crossed, the light-hearted words are spoken to somebody, somewhere for the first time: *I Must Be Getting Old*.

From that first admission, dated from that one predictable joke, self-image slips into something more comfortable. The body gives itself permission to age, subtly, and to slacken off at training: an extra beer, another cigarette. *Bit Old for That One, Boys. Bit Past It*.

'Bruno — the knee is fine. The knee is not the problem.'

The two men sat together in silence, watching the remaining light leach from the sky.

'That's what I figured.'

'I know what the problem is. It's up here.' Mack tapped his head. 'But knowing doesn't seem to help.'

'You just need a coupla games under your belt. Get some confidence.' More slow thinking, then a conclusion: 'You should talk to Aldo. He's the real boss. Get you back into the team through the back door.'

Lisa arrived with a mound of glistening fettuccine-worms, and a bowl of red sauce freckled with olives, red chillies and capers.

'*Puttanesca,*' she announced. 'A special treat for you Gentlemen.'

The words were spoken pleasantly, but aimed at her husband. He grinned, amused, but Bruno missed the joke.

'Prostitute's sauce,' she translated his parents' language for him.

Still the connection failed to register.

'I'll get the bowls,' Mack said. 'And some vino.'

2

'If it was up to me, Mack, you'd be the first player picked.'

'So who's the boss? You or Colby?'

'The committee, Mack. The committee.'

The two men sat in the stand, watching junior training. Aldo craned his head forward to sip at his Campari, holding it well clear of his silk tie.

'You know what the committee thinks about the coach, Mack?'

'The sun shines out of his arse?'

'Three wins in a row,' he pronounced. 'That's what the committee thinks. Three wins in a row.'

He sipped again, fastidiously. Mack reached out and flipped the beautiful tie between his thumb and finger, trying to expose the hidden label, half-hoping to find the words Woolworths, or Target.

'Nice tie.'

'Ermenegildo Zegna.' Aldo sipped again, giving himself time to think. 'Results, Mack. Results are what interest the committee.'

He turned his attention back to the players.

Approaching Aldo at junior training had seemed Mack's best chance for a full and frank discussion. The pleasure of watching his chubby son at play would surely lift the father into a more sentimental and generous frame of mind. The two men sat at the far end of the stand, some distance from the clumps of Dads. Aldo's Campari was empty, Mack's beer still brimming. Drinking was the last thing on his mind.

'The points are on the board,' Aldo told him. 'Our best start for years.'

'It won't last.'

Aldo snorted, irritated, and waved an impatient hand. 'What do you want us to do? Sack him?'

'Talk to him.'

'Listen, Mack. Maybe I agree with you. Don't quote me — but maybe Colby was a mistake. But what can I do? He's got a contract.'

The juniors were clustered about their coach at the far end of the pitch. Their voices glided across the flat turf as if across water: variably loud, unevenly breaking, new instruments not yet tuned. Big boys, all of them — already taller than their immigrant fathers — most were probably true under–14s, their size due to physical precocity, or better nutrition. Identity papers and birth-certificates had become *de rigeur* in the world of junior soccer; only a minority of so-called Under–14s still risked driving their own cars to matches.

At the near end of the pitch a smaller, thinner boy — the same boy, Mack realised, that he had seen before — was kicking a ball into the empty net. Fetching it out and kicking it back in. Fetch, and kick. Aldo, finding a focus for his irritation, stood and shouted.

'Hey! You! I tell you before — clear off!'

Mack touched his arm. 'He's not doing any harm.'

Aldo sat again, carefully. 'He wants to use the facilities, he can join the Club.'

'Maybe no one asked him.'

The boy and his ball disappeared, but the argument continued. It was the argument they had begun with, an argument more about Mack than the boy, relocated onto this proxy battlefield.

'Aldo — if he wants to play you should let him.'

'He's a trouble-maker. Things go missing from the bar.'

'You see him take them?'

'And the graffiti out front …'

'You *see* him?'

'Gino tried to talk to him. Get him to clean all that shit off the wall. The next day — Gino's car has these scratches down the side.'

'He admitted he did it?'

Aldo gestured behind, towards the other fathers. 'Anyway, they don't want him in the team. He doesn't fit in.'

The dark, portly fathers were scattered in groups in

the stand, drinking, chatting, watching their cherubim out on the grass. Many more were jammed around tables inside the smoke-filled Club rooms, arguing over endless card games of *Scopa* and *Sette-e-mezzo* — Broom and Seven-and-a-half — and endless glasses of brandy or *grappa*. Ostensibly waiting for their sons to finish, at the end of training they usually managed to keep the sons waiting for another round or two.

Aldo picked up the tube of *Baci* on the bench beside him, shook two out and handed one to Mack. 'How's the knee?'

'Good enough for the starting line-up.'

The Chairman nodded, distractedly; out on the pitch his big, chubby son was lining up for a shot at goal. Mack leaned forward into his field of view, forcing eye contact.

'*Vengo con il mio cuore in mano,*' he said, with some force.

Aldo snorted. 'What's that, something you read from the chocolate wrapper?'

'I come with my heart in my hand,' Mack translated, unnecessarily.

Aldo shook his head. 'Shit, Mack. I love you like a brother. We all do. But you can quote the old man till you're blue in the face — it won't change nothing. He would be the first to tell you, there's no favourites in picking the team. It's business.'

'Let's talk business then. I'm the most expensive player you've got. And I'm not playing …'

'Glad you brought that up. Now if it was just me, I'd be happy for you to stay in the house rent free. But the committee …'

Mack rose without answering and left him sitting there, astonished. He hurried through the Club rooms, seething, and out into the carpark, jammed his key into the door-lock of his car — then paused. Aldo's sky-blue Alfa was parked in the next space. He stepped across the narrow gap and pressed the sharp edge of the key to the side panel of the Alfa, but found himself unable scratch it.

'*Terrone!*' he hissed. Southerner. And kicked the front tyre instead.

From somewhere came the feeling that he was being watched. He turned to see the boy staring from the nearby shadows. With a grin on his face? The boy looked quickly away, and began juggling a soccer ball with his feet. Mack felt no shame at being caught; he was too angry for shame. He found instead a small comfort in the unspoken collusion — and took pleasure, also, in the sight of this child and his tricks: volleying the ball against the nearby wall, catching the rebound in his curved instep and holding it there, flipping it up to balance on his raised thigh. The boy's hair was loose today, parted in the middle: a thin, flapping towel on each side of his face. The thin, spiderlimbed body, revelling in its easy coordinations, still seemed undernourished. A Nail.

The ball rose again from the ground, as if self-propelled, and became stuck to the point of the boy's forehead, performing seal fashion. He was showing off, unaware that Mack already knew how good he was, that a single touch of foot on ball, a single caress, was enough.

'Where did you learn to do that?'

The ball dropped again; the boy killed the bounce beneath the sole of his sneaker. *Property of Adelaide Napoli S.C.* was stencilled on the white leather panels of the ball.

'Your brothers teach you?'

The answer was flat, matter-of-fact. 'I'm the oldest.'

'Your Dad play the game?'

'He don't live with us.'

His eyes had already left Mack's; he was nudging the ball restlessly from instep to instep. Circumnavigating the Gulf of Taranto. The man felt some sympathy for the boy. No, more than that. He felt *simpatia* — one of the first wog words he had learnt from Beppe, a sound into which the old man had breathed deep resonance. The Dads had not wanted Mack in the same team with their darlings either. Lacking a representative in the parliament of fathers, he had spent half a season stranded on the sideline, juggling a spare ball endlessly with his feet, fidgeting to and fro within view of the coach.

Beppe had forced his inclusion.

Mack stood looking at the boy, half-amused, half-disturbed by the symmetry, the echo.

'What's your name?'

'Shaun.'

'You live round here?'

The boy — Shaun — pointed vaguely up the road. 'Henry Street.'

'I don't know you from school.'

'I don't go much.'

The words were mumbled downwards, at the ball, still moving between his feet, or rolled like a lump of dough between the sole of one foot and the ground. He glanced up again. 'You gunna be our new milkie?'

'How did you know?'

'Everyone knows.'

Mack unlocked the door of the car, and climbed in. Shaun tapped at the window as he turned his key in the ignition; he wound it down.

'You playing on Saturday, Mack?'

'It's Mr McNeil to you.'

The kid grinned, not caring. 'They call you Mack at the Club, don't they?'

'They call me lots of things.' Depending, he almost added, on who I am.

The boy's grin became more angular, and even more

ugly, a lean, feral grin which marked him apart from the cute race of children. He was the opposite of cute: he was everything that cute was not.

'What do they call you?' Mack asked.

The boy jerked a thumb towards the brick wall of the Club. 'That's my tag.'

Mack turned to examine the graffiti spray-painted in black across the high cream wall. A Beppe-phrase came back from childhood, a reassurance whenever Mack would limp from the field with a barked shin or knee. *È solo un graffio.* It's just a scratch. It might have been fun to tell that to Aldo, about his precious Alfa. The darker scratches on the smooth, brick skin of the Club were in fact a single graffito, one word repeated, as if chalked a hundred times on a blackboard in an attempt to get it right. The letters were difficult to make out, a stylised script of sharp-edged runes, as angular as the boy himself. It might have been a name, it was meaningless enough to be a name, but it wasn't Shaun. *Scut.* Perhaps *Skeam.*

The graffitist was juggling his ball again between various bony points. Uncertain what to say, Mack tossed over the foil-wrapped chocolate he was still holding, quite deliberately, playing now with those echoes from his own childhood. The kid caught the chocolate with casual ease. 'Don't eat it, read it,' Mack said, and drove off without explanation.

3

Lisa was curled on the bed at home, foetal position, wrapped in a quilt. Tears streaked her face, crumpled tissues littered the surrounding carpet.

'It came?' Mack said.

'It even came *early*.'

He sat on the edge of the bed, wondering what to say. *We'll try again. There's always next month. Don't bottle it up.* How many times could a clumsy consolation be uttered, and still have meaning?

Lisa spoke instead. 'You know — the nuns at school used to say …'

The flow of her words was halting, broken by small catches in her breath.

'They used to say — the blood was the tears — of the womb.'

He placed a hand on her shoulder, and rubbed, gently. The scene had been repeated, monthly, since the miscarriage. Time had healed nothing; each month the same wound opened again, bleeding heavily, and actual tears flowed from her eyes.

But if those tears were heavier each month, their

duration was briefer. He knew that after a good cry she would rise from the bed, and carry on, toughened, as if it had never happened.

'I really think you should look into it properly. You should see someone. *We* should see someone. A specialist.'

She plucked a fresh tissue from a box on the pillow and wiped her eyes. 'Mack — we *got* pregnant, remember? There's nothing wrong. It's just timing. But it's so … frustrating.'

She covered his hand with hers. The tips of her fingers looked red raw.

'I still think you should see someone. Something might have gone wrong since.'

'It was only eighteen months ago.'

'Something might have gone wrong since,' he repeated, stubbornly.

She rolled away from him, out of reach, facing the wall.

'It's like some sort of cottage medicine. Taking your temperature every morning. There must be more you can do. Special tests.'

'I don't want tests,' she said. 'Those clinics treat you like a piece of meat. It's all so … invasive.'

'You sound like Anthea.'

She didn't answer. Another hitch in her breath, the last echo of a sob, reminded him of the more important issue.

'We can try again,' he said.

He lay down on the bed, and wrapped his arms around her, and pressed the length of his body against hers.

'We can try again now.'

'You've got to be joking.'

'It might cheer you up.'

She shifted a little further from him on the bed, once again removing herself from contact, but this time turning to face him, angry.

'Is that all you think it takes? Is that all you can think of? How very sensitive!'

He sat up, angry himself.

'It would sure cheer *me* up! The only time you're interested these days is when that fucking thermometer starts to rise!'

'That's not true. You know that's not true.'

'Maybe not — but the miscarriage didn't just affect you.'

'Mack — you don't even *want* children!'

'But I want *you*. Maybe I'm insensitive to your needs — but maybe you're insensitive to mine.'

She turned to look at him, breathing slowly and deeply, forcing herself to stay calm.

'I'm sorry if I've given that impression.'

Another pause, another slow, deep breath, as if she could inhale calmness like some kind of aerosol drug.

'Maybe I'm getting a bit …'

He was ready with the word: 'Obsessive?'

'If you like.'

He pushed himself up from the bed and walked out into the kitchen, seeking his own favourite tranquillising drug. He opened the fridge: no beer. He tapped wine from a cask into two glasses. The ritual served as a further Time Out; she looked more relaxed when he returned.

'The *fucking* thermometer?'

He grinned. 'Unintended joke.'

She propped herself upright against the head of the bed and they sat together, sipping, knowing already that the phrase, the entendre, would become a permanent addition to their private language.

'I still think you should see someone,' he said. 'It's been too long.'

'There's nothing wrong, Mack. It's just bad luck. Bad timing.'

'Maybe it's me.'

'Of course it's not you. How could it be you?'

'Maybe I should have some sort of test. Count the tadpoles.'

'Sweetheart — we *know* you've got tadpoles. It worked before, it'll work again.'

But to Mack there seemed something wilful about her insistence; she seemed too much to be arguing with herself, refusing to consider other possibilities. He found himself putting arguments *for* her, and against himself.

'Maybe I haven't got enough tadpoles. Maybe they haven't learnt to swim.'

She laughed, briefly. 'Sounds very scientific.'

'That's my point — we need someone who knows about these things.'

'Not yet,' she said. 'Please, Mack. We'll give it a few more months.'

And she rose from the bed, and checked her face matter-of-factly in the mirror of her dresser. She ran a hand once through the punk-thatch of hair, wiped away the last tears, and was ready to face the world outside the bedroom again.

4

Mack had never been a student. Schoolwork — bookwork — had been beyond him as a boy, or beyond his powers of concentration. His worst subject had been English. Paralysed by the empty pages of his exercise books, he had excelled only at the oral composition of jokes, the one-liner aimed at the teacher's back. He had shown promise at mental arithmetic: short and sharp, and either right or wrong. There was something physical about the subject that appealed to him, something akin to weightlifting. Mathematical tasks were best performed in quick, energetic sets, and almost unconsciously, moving numbers around instead of iron.

'He's very quick,' his teachers repeated to his mother on Parent Interview Night. 'Very quick. But.'

Teaching arithmetic himself was another matter. Knowing the answers spoilt the fun, spoilt the *only* fun there was. He felt a huge impatience as he stood at the blackboard each day in class, stating the obvious, or wasted his evenings marking test papers filled with identical stupid mistakes, as if the answers had been xeroxed along with the questions.

Lisa's stubborn refusal to solve her own problem irked him for the same reason. It didn't add up. Once he would have let the matter rest, privately relieved by yet another failure to conceive. He didn't want children. If pressed he would say he was not *ready* for children. But there was something irrational about her behaviour that was beginning to grate. Surely it was simple: problem, solution. Why couldn't she see that?

He made the doctor's appointment without telling her, excusing the deception with the knowledge that his motives were unselfish, and completely in her interest. The visit was an exercise in problem solving, perhaps, but more importantly, he hated to see her unhappy. He had been content to let her plough on with the monthly temperature charts, and an occasional astrology prediction, read aloud over breakfast. He had even let a visit to a clairvoyant in the Hills, recommended by Anthea, pass without much comment.

'I don't believe in it either,' Lisa defended herself at the time. 'But there's nothing to *lose*.'

Despite such measures, her unhappiness did not pass.

The doctor, elderly and frail, with a wizened, red-skinned face — more medicine man than doctor — saw through Mack immediately.

'She doesn't know you're here?'

His manner was amused rather than suspicious, but Mack stuck to his story. 'She was supposed to meet me here. Something must have come up.'

The doctor eyed him, clearly sceptical. 'It's difficult to discuss this without Lisa present. I prefer to treat the couple.'

'I thought — you could just give us some advice. I could pass it on.'

Mack produced Lisa's temperature charts, filched from her bedside drawer, as proof.

'She's been taking her temperature. She wanted you to look at these …'

The doctor accepted the charts and nodded. 'I thought I remembered talking to her about it. But that was a year or so back.'

'Fifteen months. They're all there.'

A faint smile. 'I see.'

He perched a pair of reading glasses on his nose, and leafed through the sheaf of graphs, giving each a cursory glance.

'She's certainly ovulating.'

'Then it must be me?'

The reading glasses were removed. 'Unlikely, given that she has been pregnant.'

He opened Lisa's case notes and flipped through, lips tightly compressed, as if to prevent the escape of any confidential information. When they parted, it was to confirm this: 'I really can't discuss Lisa's medical history without her permission.'

'You can discuss *me*. It might be me.'

The doctor shrugged, and flipped shut the folder. 'We always do a sperm count first. Start the ball rolling — so to speak.'

He paused, waiting for some reaction to the weak pun. Then shrugged and continued. 'It's the easiest test. Also, the cheapest. A formality, probably. But it should be done. At least before more invasive procedures.'

'And the miscarriage?'

'Your count might be low. Sub–fertile, rather than infertile. You might need more spins of the dice. Takes a little longer to get lucky …'

Mack interrupted before another pun emerged. 'How do I get them counted? Pump them out Indian file?'

A plump finger indicated a back door. 'You go through there. With a specimen bottle.'

'Now?'

The doctor nodded. He opened a drawer in a stainless steel cabinet, and took out a small plastic container with a yellow cap. From another drawer came a compact, glossy magazine. *Pocket Playgirls.*

'Try page 23,' he said. 'If you're looking for inspiration.'

'It works for you?' Mack asked, but there was no response. The door opened into some kind of treatment room: a high, central couch, a sink, glass cabinets of phials and bottles, what looked like a heart machine or monitor.

'Take your time. No one will disturb you.'

'I always take my time.'

The door closed. Mack turned to lock it, but could find neither lock nor latch. He felt absurdly exposed. He sat on the edge of the bed, in the middle of the room, and stared at the insecure door. Voices were murmuring beyond; the doctor, incredibly, was seeing another patient. Play with his cock, here, now? He remembered sometimes standing at the urinal as a kid, in the Club, when a stranger would step up onto the block next to him, and a thick gush of piss would instantly hose against the wall. Thoroughly intimidated, Mack would be unable to start.

Now he leafed through the magazine, but without yet unzipping. Each page was a variation on the same themes: big breasts, spread legs, and the unfocused fuzz of pubic hair, blurred into something softer and silken-looking. He felt no arousal. He turned to page 23 as instructed. A beach beauty was stretched, back arched, beneath a bright umbrella. She wanted him, Mack, clearly — she wanted anyone — but again he failed to respond. The over-large breasts were an absurd distraction, an engineering feat that was more puzzling than exciting. Rigid, heavy globes, clearly implanted, they would surely drag her immediately to the bottom of the ocean that glittered in the background.

He turned the page. Another naked beauty was sitting on a piano keyboard for some reason. She was holding a sheet of music; he turned the magazine sideways but couldn't read the title of the piece. Was she playing chopsticks with her cheeks? There was something hard and American about her little tough nose, and in the mouth that smiled without warmth. Not his type. He turned the page again. A dark-haired beauty had been restrained in fishnet, like some sort of sea-mammal. He turned again, and again, through a sequence of still lifes, with bodies draped on tiger skins, bear skins, harem cushions. He could find no image to worship uncritically. Each seemed flawed, and no sooner would something begin to stir between his legs, than he would detect the flaw, and lose interest. Was he looking for perfection, or was he looking for excuses? Was it the door behind him, unsecured — through which, unbelievably, the chatter of children carried?

Trying to concentrate on the magazine, it seemed that if the breasts were perfect, the smiles were sluttish; if the smiles were warm, the eyes were as hard as nails. He found one image that seemed his type, that contained no flaws, but his glance fell on the accompanying biography. *During the photo-shoot I couldn't wait to get home and pick up a book. I need to be constantly intellectually stimulated …* He fell instantly out of love. The apology in this irked him more than the pretension. Be yourself, he wanted to shout at the pouting face. Be proud of yourself. If you're dumb — so what? A lot of us are dumb.

He tossed the glossy booklet aside. The plastic specimen jar stood on the bed, waiting. What to do? Close his eyes and think of Lisa? The door was still unlocked. He dutifully retrieved the book and began again from the front, flipping forward from the playmates of twenty years ago towards those of the present. Still nothing was happening. Was his problem simply one of loyalty? He had never been unfaithful to Lisa, despite one or two drunken gropings at parties. Did jerking off over a girl in a soft-porn magazine qualify as infidelity? The idea seemed an insult to Lisa. A weird, amusing thought: if he ever was unfaithful, it should surely be with someone *worthy* of her. He flipped on, time-travelling, and the chronology of the pictures began to interest him more than the sexuality, the changing body shapes and styles from voluptuous to stick insect to girl-next-door and back again to volupt. He arrived in the eighties, looking for punkish styles — and some echo of Lisa that might arouse him. This notion also amused him: even in his fantasies, even in his choice of pornographic image, he was faithful. Preoccupied by his study, more historical now than sexual, he failed to hear the light tap on the door. He jumped, startled, when it was repeated, more loudly.

'Come in.'

The doctor poked his head through the door. 'No joy?'

Mack almost laughed. 'Not in the mood.'

'There's no — ah — problem, is there Mack? I mean, sexually. With you and Lisa.'

'No problem at all.'

'Why not take it home?'

'The magazine?'

A flicker of amusement. 'The specimen bottle. As long as you deliver it back first thing. Fresh. Or better still, take it to the lab yourself.'

5

'You did it without telling me?'

She was lying on the sofa when he arrived home that evening, reading a book. Her reaction was mixed: indignation that he had gone behind her back, tempered by surprise and curiosity. He lifted her legs from the sofa, sat, and placed them across his thighs like a rug.

'In fact I *didn't* do it.'

He plonked the yellow-capped specimen container onto the flat of her belly.

'I couldn't. Nothing happened. So now I have to do it in the morning. And deliver it, fresh.'

She stared at the container, and back at him.

'You really should have said.'

There was no venom in her words. She was confused, he could see, by the gesture, an unexpected gift. But also amused by his failure.

'Sorry, Lisa. But you were very stubborn.'

'So what did he say?'

'He said what you said. The problem is probably yours. But it's very easy for me to have the test. He won't look at you unless we get me out of the way first.'

He was still trying to cajole her, but it was unnecessary; the battle had been won.

She looked up at him, uncertainly. 'I suppose we might as well.'

'It's not very invasive,' he said.

She managed a small laugh. 'So tell me about your failure.'

'He sent me into this back room with a girlie magazine.'

'That's what I mean,' she said. 'They treat you like meat.' But she was still smiling, amused by the mental picture. '*Playboy* didn't help?'

'I read it for the articles.'

She laughed properly this time, loudly. 'You could take a specimen jar to the next Gentlemen's Evening.'

So even that had been forgiven.

'I needed your help,' he said. 'I needed you to show me how to do it.'

Another laugh. 'You're the one with the cock. Milk the thing. You've been having plenty of practice — or so you keep complaining.'

He guided her hand to the crotch of his jeans, swelling against the warm pressure of her legs.

'I thought — it might be better if we both did it.'

She bent towards him and kissed him lightly on the lips, the first real kiss she had offered for some time. And part of him rankled at this: a *Bacio* of flesh, not chocolate, but a reward for good behaviour nonetheless.

'In the morning, I thought you said. The specimen has to be fresh.'

'We could put it on ice tonight.'

He tried to wrap his arms around her, to enfold her, but she lowered her legs to the ground and twisted to her feet. He gripped the hem of her short leather skirt; she leaned her weight away from him, teasing.

He said, 'I might not be in the mood in the morning.'

'You're *always* in the mood in the morning.'

When he woke the next morning, she was already in the kitchen, fully dressed, sitting over breakfast at the bench, reading the morning paper. There was a coolness in her mood; had she changed her mind again? He reached over her shoulder and plonked the empty specimen jar next to her muesli.

She pushed it away, irritably. 'I'm trying to eat breakfast.'

He nuzzled her neck from behind.

'And if we have to do it,' she said. 'At least shave.'

He tried to remain patient. 'We have to do it.'

She swivelled on her stool to face him. 'I can't see the point.'

The paper with its big, simple headlines had been cast aside, but the conversation had been reduced to similar proportions.

'We *know* you have no problem, Mack.'

Once again, he was surprised by her response.

'It's nothing,' he said. 'A few seconds out of the day. I don't understand why you're still opposed. It just doesn't make sense.'

'It seems — unnecessary.'

'I'll shave,' he promised.

She brought the container to the bathroom a few minutes later.

'Sorry,' she said. 'Of course you're right.'

She smiled, and he felt an instant arousal. She couldn't help but notice.

'Six out of ten,' she said.

'Six point five,' he said. 'Seven. Seven point five …'

Lisa untied the cord of his pyjama pants, and dexterously used five soapy fingers on him until he was balanced on the edge of coming; after which it was easy to point the stiff end of his cock into the open container, and one of her warmest kisses, a kiss that was neither reward nor promise, that was nothing but itself, was enough to push him over the edge.

Lisa jammed the cap on the jar quickly, as if to prevent any attempted escape.

'Thank you,' she said, in the same tone that she had once used to thank him for the pleasure their love-making had given. He was still mystified — how could her attitude change so quickly?

'Careful,' he said. 'They look frisky.'

She held the container up to the light; they peered in, heads together. The white, translucent contents were surprisingly small in volume, a single phlegmy hawk.

'It felt like more,' he murmured.

'Looks fine to me.'

'It's not how *much* you've got,' he said, unable to resist an opening.

She waited, willing now to be pleased, however predictable the punch line.

'It's how many.'

The reluctant spread of her smile stirred him; he felt a welling of something too long in abeyance.

'And now,' he said. 'I want to do it again. Inside the woman I love.'

Their love-making was slower than in recent months, more prolonged — an end itself, rather than the mechanical means it had become. Tears of pleasure filled her eyes; for some time afterwards she clung to him, refusing to release him. Finally forced up and into the bathroom by his bladder, Mack returned after a long minute to find her still lying in bed, but with the thermometer now jammed between her lips.

'Again?' he said, incredulous.

She didn't answer. Her eyes stared, feline, at his with the directness of lust.

'I've got to get the specimen to the lab.'

She plucked the thermometer from her mouth. 'Another half an hour won't hurt.'

He climbed in beside her, and took the thermometer from her hand. 'You know why I hate this thing?'

'I thought you loved it. Your green light.'

He lay flat on his back, hands clasped beneath his head. She rested her own head on his chest, and gently rolled his penis — half-flaccid, not yet recovered from previous duties — between her palm and the hard bone of his pubis.

'My old man used to take his temperature every morning. If it was high, he was thrilled.'

Her refrain was automatic, her real interest elsewhere. 'He made the most of his illnesses.'

'He *cherished* his illnesses. Everything went into those little notebooks. Temperature, pulse. Urine. It's a wonder he didn't taste his shit every morning.'

'You say some choice things sometimes. Surely, it gave him a purpose, Mack. A goal.'

Mack laughed, harshly. 'It was his life's work. Steak for dinner whenever he won an extra percentage disability. Sparkling wine — remember the old Barossa Pearl? It was the only time I ever saw him happy.'

'You can't know what he went through in the war, Mack.'

She always defended the father against the son, however obliquely, although more to defend Mack against himself, he suspected, against his own darker side. On the subject of his father, he was difficult to stop. Rage was always close to the surface, the pent-up feelings had a life of their own.

'Weird, isn't it,' he said, 'wanting to be an invalid? Throwing a party when you get sicker.'

'Except you say he wasn't. It was only on paper.'

'But maybe that's it. All those pension tribunals and review hearings worked a kind of magic. Self-fulfilling prophecies. Crying wolf by slow degrees. Voodoo by percentage points.'

She moved herself above him, sitting astride his thighs, leaning forward, her small breasts, elongated slightly by gravity, brushing against his face, tingling the surface of his lips.

'It feels like your own disability was only temporary.'

He had in fact hardened a little, but without real desire. Now it was Mack's turn to go through the motions. It was difficult to get thoughts of his father out of his head. As Lisa worked assiduously at his re-arousal, he was time-travelling: sixteen again, promoted to the senior squad, home from the Club one summer evening after training. His father had been safely in bed, asleep; his mother crocheting something complicated in front of the TV. Voices still carried from the playing field.

Mack tipped a pile of schoolbooks from his bag and sat at the kitchen table, trying to concentrate. This was his best study time. After training his body loosened into a kind of plasticine, a dull, inert substance that might have belonged to someone else. For a few brief hours he could think clearly, at peace with his twitchy muscles.

But not tonight. His father had appeared, blinking, in the bedroom door, and taken a bottle of beer from the fridge and sat opposite.

'Your mob are making enough noise.'

He appropriated Mack's maths book as a beer coaster. When he took a sip, Mack retrieved the book and wiped away the rings of moisture with his sleeve.

'Funny,' his father said, eventually. 'In New Guinea all we ever wanted was sleep. I could drop off like that.'

He attempted to click his fingers, but only succeeded in rubbing them together, awkwardly, noiselessly. Time passed, then he picked up the thread again.

'We had tricks to keep awake on patrol. One bloke used to pull the pin from a grenade, and sit holding the lever down all night.'

He snorted and filled his glass again from the bottle. Mack should have been in bed, but he was suddenly intrigued. The war memories were far and few between: fine details, especially. Mostly his father preferred generalisations, of the kind he now returned to.

'Of course it was different in the desert. Before. Fighting against that lot.' He gestured towards the street, and the Napoli Club. 'When the dagoes were on the other side you could always get a good night's sleep.'

He stared into the brown glass of his bottle, and laughed. 'Give me a dago over a Jap anytime.'

Losing interest, Mack began to pack away his books; his father set his glass down on his school diary as if staking a further claim on his time.

'What's that stuff?'

'Asian History.'

'Christ — that'd be right.'

He drained the last dregs of his glass and leaning back in his chair, reached into the fridge behind him for another bottle. Surprisingly, he still wanted to talk.

'Get them to teach you some *real* history. Something useful. Get them to teach you the history of the Seventh Division. Get them to tell you why the poor bastards who spent years fighting dagoes in the desert in Africa thought they were coming home, but found themselves up in the jungle fighting Japs.'

He lifted his hand and the glass slipped from it, smashing on the table top. He swept the fragments aside, irritated, scattering them across the kitchen floor. His hand was now bleeding, but the injury had angered him further. He was beyond safe help in this condition. As he swore to himself in the bathroom, sluicing cold water on the injured hand, Mack retrieved the spare car keys — kept hidden beneath the kitchen sink for nights like this — woke his mother, who was dozing in front of a snowing television screen, and led her outside to the car and safety.

6

Aldo spoke with Colby as promised. The team list was pinned to the noticeboard the following Thursday, and Mack found his name above the line. But in the change room, on Saturday, the pleasure of inclusion was tarnished. As the team line-up was chalked onto the blackboard he found himself in a new role, a redundant midfield position, bypassed by Colby's long-ball tactics.

'I'm a goal-scorer,' he protested.

Colby continued chalking names and arrows onto the blackboard. Benches lined three walls of the room; the players, warmed, sinews stretched, watched like schoolkids.

'No filmstars in this team, McNeil.'

'It's what I *do*, for Christ's sake. Scoring goals.'

Colby shook his head. 'Not today, son. Work hard. Chase. Support. That's all I want. Just another day at the office.'

It was someone else's office; its rules and procedures unfamiliar. Mack ran up and back, and to and fro, and around in circles, over the middle third of the pitch, for forty-five minutes. The ball was a ping-pong high above his head, a shuttlecock always just out of reach. When he found it at his feet, more by luck than intent, he instinctively tried to slow the game down, chess-fashion, shielding the ball, feinting his way into free space. For Mack, space was a dimension of time on the soccer field. Space *was* time. Both could be expanded or contracted, the pace and movement of the game could be slowed, halted, even reversed.

Colby's terrier-bark carried from the dugout. 'It's not a bleedin' egg, McNeil! You don't have to hatch it!'

Towards the end of the half, the ball again on the ground at his feet, a chink opened in the wall of defenders in front of him. He baulked, and the chink widened into a narrow doorway; he slalomed through, finding a sudden, sweet corridor between the bodies. A moment before the door slammed shut he half-turned and chipped the ball — a high, dipping, topspun wedge-shot — over the goal-keeper's head.

A fraction too high, it scraped the cross-bar and deflected up and back into the small group of supporters beyond.

This attempt brought a shouted lecture in the change rooms at half-time.

'Ever heard of the KISS principle, McNeil?'

'Not since Under–14s.'

'Keep It Simple, Stupid!' Colby said, ignoring him.

'The *Bacio* principle,' Bruno murmured somewhere,

as if to draw some of the fire.

'You have an opinion on this, Panozzo?'

'Beppe's coaching system.'

The door was locked; Club officials huddled in the background. Someone had used the toilet cubicle in the corner and forgotten to flush. The tiny, hot room filled with sweating men stank of shit. Mack felt like retching.

Colby ranted on. 'It's a *simple* game for simple people. Up front: Move Into Space. At the back: Mark Your Man. In the middle … ' He looked Mack's way, 'First to The Ball. Early Pass. You Lose the Ball, *You* Win it Back.'

The Commandments were chalked on the board as he spoke. 'That's all there is to it. Not the Royal bleedin' Ballet — football. Right?'

There was something about the relative status of coach and team — Colby standing at the blackboard, the players faces, upturned — that rankled. Mack raised his hand, as if in class.

'Can I say something?'

'If it's constructive.'

'I think we need to keep possession more. We need to slow the game down in the middle.'

'Good point,' Bruno murmured, softly.

'You always know better, don't you, McNeil?'

Mack stood, deliberately; his head was now above Colby's, speaking down. 'Are you watching this game?

Or are you watching some game in your fucking head? They're running all over us in the middle.'

No one spoke. He hadn't meant to raise his voice, the words seem to shout themselves.

'Take an early shower,' Colby finally told him, coldly.

'Bullshit. You can't win it without me.'

Mack glanced to Aldo, standing in the doorway, for support; the Chairman shrugged his shoulders, saying nothing. Across the room, Bruno was shaking his head: a told-you-so look. A gone-too-far look. *Vai sempre oltre i limiti.*

Colby glanced from face to face in turn, lingering a little on Bruno, co-mutineer.

'Anyone else got anything to say?'

Bruno stared back, insolently, but this time keeping silent, unwilling to make a further sacrifice. He wanted to play out his last few games; the Club, finally, was where his loyalty lay. Mack rose, peeled off the powder-blue shirt — the coveted number 10, Pelé's number, Maradona's number, his since adolescence — and tossed it into the centre of the room. His blue shorts followed. After showering, he watched the remainder of the game from the players' race, still seething. Aldo brought out a beer, and stood with him.

'I want you in the team, Mack. But the coach doesn't.'

'You're full of shit, Aldo. Just fucking tell him. You think Beppe would let him get away with that stunt?'

'My dad always put the Club first.'

'He put people first. He'd be ashamed of you.'

Mack had gone too far, and knew it: invoking the father against the son.

'He'd be ashamed of *you*,' Aldo said. 'He'd tell you to grow up! *Non fare il bambino!*'

Stop being the boy. The words of the old man, even from beyond the grave, calmed Mack a little. Or was it the melody, the familiar, soothing cadence of the language?

'I'm sorry, mate. I was over the top.'

'So what's new? I understand you're pissed off, Mack, but Colby's the boss. I can lean on him — but it has to be done subtly. Be patient.' He smiled. 'Your turn will come. *Un pranzo comprende molte pietanze.*'

Another Beppe-phrase: a meal consists of many dishes. Mack countered with his own.

'Better an egg today than a hen tomorrow.'

The exact Italian was beyond him: *È meglio l'uovo oggi?* The approximate meaning, at least, was clear: an egg in the hand is worth a bird in the bush.

Reassured, Aldo headed off in search of other company. Equanimity wasn't easy for Mack; not even the chocolate-coated music of Italian could soothe him for long. As he watched the match his frustration flared

185

again; soon it was uncontrollable. When his replacement — Watson, the skin — scored the winning goal with a free kick against the run of the play he was so disgusted that he smashed his fist hard against the side of the stand.

'Fucking fig jam!'

Anger masked the pain in his hand for a time, but soon he was grimacing, nursing his wrist. In silence Aldo drove him to the hospital at speed, braking his Alfa in the emergency bay as if it were a compact ambulance.

'I have to get back,' he said, reaching into the glove box, from where he pulled out a Cabcharge pad, and gently detached a voucher. 'This is for your trip home. Ring the Club if there are any problems. Okay?'

'I'll be fine.'

He rested his hand on Mack's arm for a moment. 'All the committee agree, Mack — we want you in the team.'

Mack stared him in the eye.

He returned the stare, unwaveringly, and the unspoken question. '*I* want you in the team. I swear.'

He was telling the truth, Mack sensed immediately — if not the whole truth. The words were uttered with a shade too much conviction; a false note jarred, subliminally. And then he saw it, at least in part: Aldo was relieved to be able to tell the truth. But that relief obscured something else, a larger story.

He puzzled over this while sitting, abandoned, in the hospital waiting room, but could arrive at no simple answer. The X-rays confirmed a small broken bone somewhere in the fleshy base of the thumb, a tiny bird-bone, painful out of all proportion to its size. He arrived home, by taxi, hand and forearm sheathed in a lightweight fibreglass cast.

'Again?' was Lisa's dry comment.

She was slicing vegetables at the kitchen bench, wrapped in an apron, her orange hair, growing longer, hoisted into a casual spout. She barely glanced at his arm as he eased its strange, altered weight onto the bench top. The sequence of snaps and cracks and breakages that had begun in his teens had long since exhausted her reservoirs of sympathy.

'It's nothing much,' he murmured.

'What about the milk round?'

'I'll manage. It's lighter than plaster. Fibreglass. Very hi-tech.'

He took a beer from the fridge, and escaped outside. The sun had vanished, the heat had piled clouds up into high thunderheads. The dull rumble of thunder carried to him for the first time that year. Towards the west, beyond the Club, the flickering of lightning could be seen, connecting cloud to ground.

Lisa poked her head out through the door. 'I'd better bring in the washing. Give me a hand?'

'I can give you one.'

The ghost of a smile. 'Better than none. I wouldn't ask — but I don't think there's much time.'

He followed her through the house, and out onto the steep back slope. The sky was suddenly dark above them, the air very still. The pegged socks, shirts and knickers hung from the line like a row of stiff pennants.

'Anthea rang about the quiz night,' Lisa said as they worked.

'Another quiz night?'

'Saturday week.'

Thunder rumbled again, more loudly, almost overhead, and the first rain of autumn began to splatter down, big, plump drops plopping noisily onto the ground. Lisa unpegged the clothes more quickly. He tried to keep up, working with his good hand, clutching the clothes as they dropped between the fibreglass plaster and his chest.

'She wanted to check with you first,' Lisa said. 'See if you're available.'

'I'm available — if she asks nicely.'

'She wants the same team. Cover all possibilities. She needs you especially.'

'It's good to know my station in life,' he said. 'Who won the 1962 Melbourne Cup? Name the winner of the hundred metres' gold medal at the Seoul Olympics …'

Her mouth full of pegs, Lisa said nothing as he

rambled on. And so they worked away from each other, from the centre of the line outwards, unclipping the clothes, tossing them hastily into the basket, as the long summer ended.

7

Growing old was not a gradual process, it seemed to Mack — more a slow, steady decline, following some gentle glide-path. A flight of stairs was the better analogy. A quick step down, steady as she goes for a time, perhaps even one step back up, then two steps down again.

Downwards into darkness, of course — but in the interludes, the suspended Time Out of each level landing, it was possible to pretend that not much was happening. It was possible to slow the pace of the game, to find a little extra breathing space.

The small bones of his body had taken turns to fracture over the years, passing the same white casing of plaster from limb to damaged limb like some thick, heavy relay baton. A change in the weather always rekindled those old aches, as did moments of sexual climax, when his war-wounds glowed with a more pleasurable pain, becoming temporary erogenous zones. At those times it seemed as if his body was remembering every fracture and injury it had ever received, in an agony of nostalgia.

190

'You tell him, Mother,' Lisa said. 'He shouldn't be playing at his age.'

'Injuries happen at any age,' he said, mildly.

They sat at a tiny table in a corner of the day room, eating the cake that Lisa had brought for his mother's birthday, and sipping tea from delicate rose-patterned china, carried out from her room.

'Delicious,' his mother said. 'I don't know how you have the time, dear.'

'I bought the cake, Mother.'

An expression of surprise. 'It's very nice cake — for bought cake.'

Mack, using his free hand, forked the last crumbling piece up and in. 'Could someone cut me another slice?'

Lisa laughed. 'You just want to be the centre of attention,' she said, but reached across and sliced the cake.

His mother was an ever-reliable source of sympathy. 'Does it hurt, dear?'

'Aches a bit at night.'

'And at other times,' Lisa added.

A television droned in another corner of the day room, unwatched. A woman in a wheelchair had been planted in front of it, like a child, baby-sat electronically. Her sleeping head had rolled to one side, drool leaking from a corner of her open mouth, strands of sticky web connecting chin to shoulder. Mack averted his eyes, but not his ears. *Jackpot bonus question for the carry-over champion,* a glib voice gabbled. *Name the capital city of Brazil.*

'Rio,' he said out loud.

Brasilia, the quiz show host corrected him.

'You should go on it,' his mother said, deaf to the correct answer. 'You always know the answers.'

'He knows the sports questions,' Lisa said, and caught his eye, another private tease.

The mention of sport returned his mother's thoughts to an earlier track. 'So are you going to keep playing, dear? When the cast comes off?'

'Of course he is, Mother. He'll play till he drops.'

Lisa still adopted a tone of affectionate amusement when discussing such things with others. In private, the amusement had vanished.

'I don't know yet,' he lied, but the women weren't listening, they had already decided for him, between them.

Name the five Great Lakes of North America …

'Superior. Michigan,' he said, then halted. 'I used to know this. Ontario.'

'Erie,' Lisa added, then waited while the compere supplied the last. *Huron.*

They turned towards the TV, trying to out-guess each other, a competition to pass the time.

Mystery bonus-board question. Who am I …

'Cleopatra,' Lisa guessed, absurdly.

I was born in 1922 ....

They both laughed. 'Don Bradman,' Mack tried.

... in a small town in France. I was educated at ...

'Is everything alright at school, dear?' his mother asked.

'Up and down.'

'It's only a few blocks away. But I never see him, Lisa. When he was teaching on the other side of town I used to see him more.'

'He's very busy,' his wife defended him.

'Flat out like a lizard drinking,' he said, using an old phrase of his father's.

If his mother noticed she gave no indication. 'I do love visitors,' she said. 'I hardly get out.'

Her criticism, already oblique, was deflected even further by Lisa. 'But you have your friends here, Mother. You have the day trips ...'

The older woman turned back to the quiz show. The television was some distance off, but perhaps offered relief from the urge to answer her daughter-in-law honestly.

'If you get up early enough,' Lisa said, 'you'll see plenty of him soon.'

Mack glared at her above his mother's bent back, and vigorously shook his head; he wasn't yet ready to confess to the milk round.

193

'We'd better get moving,' he said.

'But you just got here, dear.'

'Sorry, Mum. I'll stay longer next time. We're due out.'

This, oddly, brightened her mood. She liked to hear news of their social life, as if, trapped in her prison, she could live it with them, vicariously.

'You're always so busy,' she said, without disapproval. 'Where are you going tonight?'

'A quiz night.'

At this coincidence, his mother managed a laugh, or at least a smile with sound effects, her first for the day. It allowed Mack to feel less guilty about abandoning her as he followed Lisa down the long corridor. In fact, he mostly felt relief: a younger and healthier world waited beyond the exit; he glanced neither left nor right into the other chambers of the nursing home, preferring not to know.

8

The surrounds of Anglican Girls' Grammar were less Volvo Belt than Range Rover Belt. Or so it seemed to Mack. The number of four-wheel drive wagons parked around the school hall was surely greater than could have been found in the entire outback of South Australia. The school parents dismounting from their Rovers and Land Cruisers and Nissan Patrols and Jeep Cherokees were dressed as if their four-wheeled vehicles were still four-legged: jodhpurs or stirrup-pants for the uniformly blonde women, the men in moleskins, elastic-sided boots and even the odd Akubra, although the sun had long gone. The geography was wrong — these were the eastern suburbs of Adelaide, not the northern *regioni* of Italy — but the word seemed a good fit: polenta-eaters. No: *lotus*-eaters.

Anthea's three-door Rav, a cute designer four-wheel drive, was a toy version of its big cousins, and even more pretentious in Mack's eyes. She waved, tugging a hamper from the raised hatchback as he crawled past, searching for a parking spot.

'What's she think? She's going to get bogged in the

David Jones carpark?'

Lisa laughed, but defended her friend. Moving from the public system to a private school had brought her deeply into Anthea's field of force; her opinions had shifted correspondingly.

'They're just family cars, Mack. Safe for children.'

She hasn't got any children, he almost said — but managed to hold his tongue.

They lifted out their own basket of nibbles and bag of drinks and followed Anthea into the hall, a vast, carved cedar barn lined with framed portraits of former school headmistresses and gilt-lettered Honour Boards of sporting and scholastic achievement.

Mary and Iain were already seated, heads together over an anagram sheet, scribbling answers. A newcomer to the team, a young girl, a pimple-faced teenager, also sat at the table, but slightly to one side, as if uncertain of her place in things.

'My niece Emma,' Anthea said. 'Did I tell you? Nick and Tina couldn't make it.'

The girl smiled hesitantly, avoiding eye contact. A loner, Mack sensed, with nothing better to do on a Saturday night.

'How will we manage without Tina?' Lisa said.

'That's why I asked Emma. She can cover for Tina.'

Mack doubted it. Tina's area of quiz night expertise was pop trivia: song lyrics, film credits, Hollywood names and dates and divorces. Emma — bookish, bespectacled, her teeth in metal shackles — looked far too unworldly. Introductions over, Anthea arranged the seating: Lisa at her side, Mack wedged between Emma and Mary. Wine was uncorked, cling-wrap detached from the first platters of nibbles. The position of team scribe was decided on precedent: Anthea re-elected, unopposed. The designated 'runner' — the team member whose task was to carry the completed answers to the marking desk as speedily as possible after each round of questions — was also decided on precedent. All eyes turned to Mack, if with some irony.

'How's the plaster?' Iain asked.

'Fibreglass. Don't even know it's there.'

'And the knee?'

'It can get me to the front table and back.'

'Any other injuries we don't know about?'

Mack laughed. 'You want a fitness test? A medical certificate?'

Mary, casting a knowledgeable eye over the assembling multitude, suddenly leant forward and hissed, in a whisper, 'They're here.'

The niece, Emma, looked puzzled. 'Who are here?'

'The professionals. Don't look now — three tables back.'

In unison, all turned and looked. The object of their attention, a team of four couples at a table towards the rear of the hall, stood and waved back, shaking their fists in mock-hostility.

'Trip up their runner as he comes past,' Mack suggested to Emma. 'I'll use my elbows if it comes to the crunch.'

'Deck him with your fibreglass,' Iain said.

'You men,' Mary said, amused.

Mack turned on her. 'What do you mean — you men?'

'She means you're all the same,' Anthea put in.

'You think Iain and I are the same?'

'Deep down, yes.'

'Thanks, Anthea,' Iain said. 'But no thanks.'

Mack turned on his friend, mock-incredulous. 'You don't want to be me? You should be flattered!'

They all laughed; Mack refilled his wine glass, and offered another glass to Emma. She was below the legal drinking age, surely, but he wanted to make her feel at home. He wanted also to treat her like a woman — this plain, plump girl forced to socialise with relatives.

'What excuse did Nick and Tina come up with?' he asked.

Anthea turned to Lisa, surprised. 'You haven't told him?'

'He's been a bit preoccupied.'

Mack guessed immediately. 'When did it happen?'

'Last week. Of course it was on the cards.

Remember the last quiz night? They were hardly talking to each other.'

'She finally outgrew him,' Mack said, and Lisa promptly kicked him beneath the table, locating his shin unerringly among the tangle of wooden and human legs.

'Who are the professionals?' Emma still wanted to know.

'Our sworn enemies,' Mack said. 'They call *us* the professionals.'

Anthea explained further. 'Traditional rivals. They win one quiz night. We win the next.'

'You sound like you take it heaps seriously.'

'No pressure at all,' Mack told her. 'We'll just rip your ears off if you don't know the tunes.'

The girl laughed, less uncertainly; he topped up her wine glass, and refilled his own.

'The women take it seriously,' he said. 'Iain and I aren't really into that female horn-locking thing.'

He grinned at Lisa, inviting another kick; she poked out her tongue instead. Anthea was laughing. Sometimes she seemed to respond to his jokes, sometimes not.

Mary turned. 'Hush, children. They're about to start.'

A butter-voiced compere had applied his mouth to the microphone and announced a game of heads-and-tails, 'to break the ice'. Anthea hustled her team to its feet, and efficiently allocated roles: both hands on head, or both hands on tail, or one hand on each, according to mathematical probability. The compere tossed two coins, a head and a tail.

Half the team sat. After three further tosses, Lisa was still on her feet, along with four other survivors scattered through the hall, one at the table of their rivals.

A sudden death playoff; Lisa sat, eliminated. The first prize of the night — half a dozen bottles of wine — was won by the professionals.

'Shitty vintage,' Iain declared, as their runner, a jovial red-faced bear of a man, squeezed past. 'I wouldn't cook with it.'

Returning a few moments later with his prize, their adversary reached over and dumped it in the middle of the table.

'Our compliments,' he said, smugly. 'We win so much of this stuff we can't get through it.'

The first question was read out, the first of ten in a round of geography.

'An easy one to start with,' the compere announced. 'What is the name of the third planet from the sun?'

Mack thrust his arm into the air, repeatedly, in schoolboy fashion. 'Miss! Miss! I know that one. Ask me, Miss Pridmore. I know the answer.'

Anthea laughed again.

'Question two — name the driest continent on that planet.'

'Oz, surely,' Iain said.

Emma leant forward urgently. 'I think it's a trick question.'

All eyes turned to her, surprised.

'The answer might be Antarctica.'

Mack laughed. 'You've got to be kidding.'

'No — think about it. It's completely dry. Ice, yes — but no water. It snows, but it never rains.'

'You've got my vote,' Anthea said, and crossed out her previous answer. 'You agree, Mack?'

Mack filled the girl's glass again, a reward. She was beaming, relaxed now. Somewhere in the hall, a mobile phone chirped.

'That's how the professionals do it,' Mack told her. 'They've got someone sitting by the phone at home with *Encyclopedia Britannica*.'

Emma laughed, obligingly. He could feel the pressure of her thigh against his beneath the table — accidentally, surely. The questions continued from the compere, progressively more difficult. The last of the geography segment, amazingly, was to name the five Great Lakes of North America. Each team member seemed to know at least three — but the same three. Mack and Lisa said nothing as further discussion retrieved a fourth, lodged in some communal memory, as if each brain had memorised only a piece of the name, a single syllable. Lisa held her tongue and allowed

Mack to name the fifth, a small, if bogus, triumph. He grabbed the completed sheet from under Anthea's nose, and it was the first slapped down on the marking desk, earning a bonus prize, a slab of chocolate.

Returning to his team, he was greeted like a hero with high-fives and backslaps, an exaggerated, comic display intended mostly for their rivals.

'Give *them* the chocolate,' Iain urged, and Mack turned and tossed the slab high over the intervening tables to the table of their rivals, where it was deftly caught, and immediately thrown back.

Another game of heads-and-tails followed. Anthea urged a new tactic.

'Do exactly what the professionals do. It'll drive them mad.'

Iain said, laughing, 'I think we need to re-examine our aims and objectives.'

'Come on — it'll be fun.'

The sports questions arrived in round five. Mack missed a couple, and received no help from the rest of the team, helpless with the topic.

'You know we know nothing about sport,' Mary said.

'You love sport,' he told her. '*This* is sport. Only more dangerous.'

She laughed, easily amused.

'Anthea loves sport most of all,' he said. 'Our team coach.'

'If you want to provoke me, Mack — you'll have to do better than that.'

The challenge, however good-humoured, was not to be refused. He turned to Emma. 'You know why you're here?'

'Anthea said you needed someone for the music questions?'

That silenced him for a moment. Lisa took the opportunity to explain. 'Mack's offended because he thinks he's only invited for the sports questions.'

'I am,' he said.

'What — offended, or only invited for the sports questions?' Iain asked.

'Both.'

Anthea intervened. 'Even if you are, so what? Sport is your area of expertise — we all respect that. The only person who denigrates it is you yourself.'

'You might respect it on quiz night,' Mack said. 'But that's the only time!'

His voice was suddenly, inexplicably raised; a few faces at nearby tables had turned in their direction.

Iain whispered, urgently, 'Easy, Mack.'

The enemy runner squeezed past again, carrying cups of coffee. 'This some new tactic, people? You trying to distract us with a little internal discord?'

Mack, chastened, held his tongue for a time. Without his input conversation seemed to flag, a mood of awkwardness settled over the team. Not even the next round of questions offered an escape; suddenly there were gaps in their collective knowledge. Falling further behind their rivals they nibbled compulsively, as if seeking comfort in the little bowls of olives and cashews or platters of paté and pressed meats and cheese spreads. Excuses and mild recriminations began to be heard around the table, mumbled through full mouths.

'I *knew* that. It was on the tip of my tongue.'

'Then you should have said.'

'Why did you change the answer?'

'We had a vote, remember? A show of hands.'

'I didn't show mine. I thought we had a policy — always go with first instinct.'

'Then you *should* have said.'

'I did. I said I had a gut feeling.'

Lisa's diagnosis — that he had ruined the evening, that his single outburst had planted the seed of later discord — would be aired on the way home, Mack knew. With force. As Anthea distributed the contents of the Second Prize hamper at the end of the evening, his thoughts were already there, in the car, preparing the usual defence. *With me, you take the good with the bad. Flipsides of the same coin. The life of the party is sometimes the death of the party.*

He could hear her reply already, a sarcastic echo: *Sometimes?* He felt suddenly, overwhelmingly tired: dead himself, emptied of life and jokes. Not even Emma's goodnight kiss on his lips — wet and open-mouthed, tasting of wine and cheese-dip — lifted him. His knee, cramped beneath the table all evening, ached; he felt bloated with snacks and wine. The sight of his portion of the loot, fancy wines, gourmet cheeses and imported chocolates, nauseated him. It all seemed so much polenta. The team failure, and the failure of the night, and his own stupid part in it, ate at him; by the time he reached the car he found himself wanting to ask for forgiveness.

And wanting also to ask what Lisa saw in him at all. Why she still stuck with him. She answered the unspoken question, obliquely, on the way home, as he babbled on, trying not to think such thoughts, trying to distract himself as much as her.

'Hurry,' he was saying. 'Drive faster. I need to get home to a good book.'

'Are you drunk again?'

'Just in need of intellectual stimulation.'

'I haven't a clue what you're talking about,' she said. 'And I don't care.'

She drove on, changing gears with unnecessary force.

'You used to make me laugh, Paul,' she said, softly. 'That's a joke in itself. I actually used to think you were *funny!*'

9

More rain fell from the sky as Mack coasted down to the Club the following Tuesday: a steady, heckling drizzle, the minimum rainfall required to ruin the enjoyment of training.

Colby revelled in the wet, reminded, perhaps, of home. The goalmouth was soon a swamp; the players' clothes and limbs splattered with mud, their boots encased in a wet, clay cladding. With the coach nagging from one direction and the sky spitting on him from another, Mack had soon had enough. His was the first excuse accepted: a wet plaster cast that was likely to soften and split.

That the cast was fibreglass and waterproof he saw no need to admit.

Shaun was waiting in the carpark as he emerged from the Club, sheltering beneath a tree from the still spitting sky. A school bag was slung over his shoulder; a cigarette glowed in his mouth.

'Give us a lift, Mack?'

'Fair go. It's just down the road.'

'No — the railway station.'

The boy tugged open the passenger door and climbed in without waiting for an answer. Despite the rain, the night was still warm, as if the heavy quilt of cloud had trapped the day's heat, refused it permission to leave. The boy was sodden; the small volume of the car filled instantly with a wet rankness; a humid mix of stale sweat and unwashed clothes. He heaved his bag into the back seat; it clanked, metallically.

'What have you got in there?'

'Homework.'

'Bit late for going into the city.'

'I'm meeting some friends.'

'At this hour?'

Mack's disapproval was more conversational than genuine; more teacher-habit. He felt an adolescent kinship with this kid, but had forgotten the language, forgotten how to talk with him.

'We ride around on the trains. Lend us ten bucks?'

'What for?'

'Something to eat. And some smokes.'

'I'll lend you five. You can forget the smokes.'

Shaun shrugged. 'I can rack some. Can I sign your plaster?'

Was this the reason Mack couldn't quite find the conversational range? The kid's words were a strange sweet-and-sour mix of the knowing and the innocent, of adult and child. Shoplifter and hero-worshipper, in one sentence. His wet T-shirt clung to his bony rib cage, as if shrink-wrapped by the rain. He needed food, certainly.

'If you want to,' Mack said. 'When we stop.'

'Didn't think you could drive with it.'

'It's awkward.'

Mack nosed the car between the high brick pillars of the Club gate, and accelerated towards the main road.

'How can you deliver the milk?'

'I haven't started yet. Next week.'

'I might help you.'

Mack laughed. 'At four a.m.? Your mother wouldn't let you.'

'If *you* don't tell her, *I* fucking won't.'

Mack was amused, enjoying, momentarily, the feeling of being one of the boys again, party to a teenage conspiracy.

'I don't think it would be a good idea,' he said, without any conviction.

His teacher self had shrunk in recent weeks, the careful classroom voice had grown weaker and fainter — but it was still there, like something perched on his shoulder, a miniature cartoon character in a mortarboard, instructing him, whispering into his ear.

Shaun was putting the opposite case into his other ear, talking for himself, needing no advocate. His wet face shone as the idea took definite shape. 'I'll climb out my bedroom window.'

'You mustn't do that,' Mack said.

'It's my *door*.'

The yellow and orange glow of a hamburger franchise — luminescent road hazard colours — glittered, waveringly, through the drizzling rain. Mack turned the car in. He had always hated Big Macs for their appropriation of his name; he felt a small satisfaction each time he patronised the opposition.

'What you doing, Mack?'

'Lending you that fiver.'

'I can't hack whoppers.'

'And I can't hack lending money unless I know where it's spent.'

A plump girl in a costume of the same road hazard colours — bright orange, lurid yellow — took the order, and the money. Her face was brick-red, pimpled, her greasy hair wrapped in a tight fishnet. Mack was reminded of the girl, Emma, on the quiz night. She looked past Mack to the boy as she passed out a compact package of food.

'Enjoy your meal.'

'Enjoy your five bucks.'

Mack laughed, warming to the boy, the quickness of his tongue, his sureness in himself.

'Worth another five?' Shaun asked, even more sure of himself.

Still amused, Mack extracted another mauve note

from his wallet. 'No spraypaint.'

'I don't *buy* spraycans.'

'You rack them?' Mack asked, trying the taste of the new word.

That he might be using it ironically didn't cross the boy's mind. He nodded, matter-of-fact. 'On principle.'

'I start at the end of your road at four,' Mack said. 'Next Monday.'

'Wicked! Could you knock on my window?'

Once again, that sweet-and-sour mix, the lingering sporting hero-worship of a child beneath the street-smart teenager.

The teacher of fifteen years was still whispering on Mack's shoulder, briefly scrupulous. 'No.'

But as they drove on, the idea of working with an assistant was growing on him.

'I could pay you,' he said. 'I remember I could always use a little extra pocket money as a kid.'

He braked the car at the lowered boom and flashing red lights of the railway crossing.

'I'll get out here,' Shaun said, suddenly fidgety, unwilling to wait.

He climbed out, then opened the back door for his bag.

'Enjoy your meal,' he said, with that now familiar feral grin.

Mack laughed, less at the joke, now well-worn, than

at the boy's cockiness as he slammed the door, and ducked under the barrier. He stepped onto the line without glancing in either direction, and walked, tight-rope fashion, balanced on one rail, towards the platform some distance off. The approaching train hooted imperiously; distracted by this small drama Mack failed to notice for some minutes the package of food abandoned on his passenger seat.

Once seen, however, he also smelt it: a warm, fatty aroma that filled the car, displacing the rankness of the boy. At the first red light he reached across, broke open the flimsy paper package, and ate.

10

Suddenly it was the season for sociability. Parties and barbecues that had been deferred, through laziness or disorganisation, now had to be rushed before the long summer gave completely. A flurry of gatherings culminated in a farewell barbecue — Mack's farewell barbecue — at Iain and Mary's.

Mack had planned to arrive on time — 'sixish' was Iain's suggestion — but it proved impossible. Lisa dropped him at the Club in the early afternoon, and he played in a losing Reserves game with his fibreglass cast in a cushion of protective foam padding, approved by the match referee. He played well, volleying in an equalising goal late in the second half. The weight of the fibreglass on his arm seemed a precise counterweight to the weakness of his left leg, providing exactly the right adjustment to body balance, restoring his timing.

The lack of pressure in the lower grade, the greater scope for individual flair, also helped. The series of dance-steps that led Mack to the goal might have been choreographed, or perhaps were beyond choreography, too much a jazz improvisation, a response to given circumstances. Mack had drawn two defenders towards him, slipped a deep diagonal ball between them to his own overlapping full-back, and sprinted to the far-post for the return pass. He swivelled mid-air and struck the incoming ball with the top surface of his foot, the sweet hard curve that Beppe liked to call Calabria.

A moment of frozen time: no one else moving as the ball tangled in the back of the net.

He sat out the Senior game on the bench and was disappointed when the team won again. After a few grudging celebratory drinks he drove Bruno home in the milk truck that was to be his for the next few months.

'Sure you're up to it?' Bruno said, referring to the fibreglass cast.

'It's fine.'

Single, thirtyish, Bruno still lived with his parents. An old joke at the Club, probably invented by Mack: he couldn't stay awake long enough to ask a girl to marry him. The house was standard Little Italy: cream-brick, geometric vegetable garden front and back, with a roadside fruit-stand to catch the passing trade. Bruno's mother was out among the cabbage-heads, dressed in black, bent double. His father was still in the Club rooms, playing *Scopa*. The house and garden were a Mediterranean cliché, but resembled nothing Mack had actually seen during his travels in Italy the year before. It looked like something from an earlier era, a postcard scene lifted from the Calabria of forty years ago, and suspended in time, in the new country.

'*Fa freddo, signora.*'

'*Un po' freddo,* Mack.'

Further weather information was exchanged as Bruno checked under the bench seat of the truck and sifted through the glove box debris, retrieving valuables.

'This must be yours,' the big man said.

He extracted a bent business card from among the clutter of pens, small change, food-wrappers, and music cassettes. Mack recognised it immediately: *Monique. Entertainment For Men.*

'It's not my fucking truck,' Mack said, laughing.

'Vince must have dropped it.'

'Anything you say, mate.'

The last item Bruno extracted was a press-seal plastic bag, bulging with greenish leaf-shreds, and a flat white pack of cigarette papers.

'A little bonus for you, Mack.'

'I don't want your stash.'

'No — keep it. Try a smoke after the round. Head down to the beach, watch the sun come up. Nothing like it.'

Mack tossed the card back into the glove box next to the sealed bag, put his foot to the clutch and turned the key in the ignition. The ageing engine spluttered once or twice, then chugged into life.

Bruno leant back through the window. 'One other thing, mate. Watch your back. There's talk.'

Mack restored the gear-stick to neutral, letting the engine idle. 'About what?'

Bruno wouldn't meet his eye. 'The team's winning without you — but Aldo wants you in the line-up. You got to ask why.'

'He owes me,' Mack said. 'He's got a lot of money invested in me.'

'It's more than that.'

Mack, puzzled, waited for more. The drinks at the Club, a warm presence in his stomach, were beginning to infiltrate more deeply; it was difficult to be concerned.

'Apparently he's really putting the screws on Colby.'

This was good news to Mack; he felt a sudden glow of brotherly affection for Aldo. 'I might have to revise my opinion of him.' He slipped the truck into gear. 'Got to go. I'm late for my funeral.'

Bruno hadn't finished. 'Listen, dickhead. If he's doing it, he's not doing it for *you.*'

Mack waited, still unconcerned, for more — but only guarded generalities were forthcoming.

'You know him better than me, Mack. You know how he thinks. But I hear things.' The big face grinned,

215

abruptly, as if trying to make light of the serious words. 'I'm not always asleep — sometimes I'm listening.'

'You talking about my house?'

'I'm not talking about nothing. Just that Aldo is a treacherous little cunt.'

Mack laughed. '*Tell* me, fuck you!'

'It's not my job. You want more, talk to Vince.'

Twenty minutes across town, the afternoon had run its course. Mack was two hours late; several of his school colleagues had already left, probably in disgust. Lisa was still present, sitting within a kraal of deck chairs and banana lounges on the back lawn. Two rickety card tables inside the perimeter upheld the remnants of the salads, and a few cold sausages on which the fat had hardened like white candlewax.

Iain glanced up, pulling his chair to one side to allow Mack entry. 'Ah — the milkman cometh.'

Lisa's face was stone. 'I've been telling everyone that you wouldn't miss a drink with the boys after the game just to get to your own farewell party. No one believed me.'

'It wasn't the drinks,' he said.

Mary intervened. 'We've saved you some food.'

'We're just glad you *got* here,' Iain said. His bow tie of the day looked hand-painted, a tiny canvas of dots and dashes, a designer morse code. 'We were beginning to get worried. Thought you must have broken another bone.'

Mack caught Anthea's eye, briefly, among the faces, and waited to hear some further criticism of his late arrival. For once she held her tongue, an outsider at this gathering of his school colleagues.

He said, apologetically hearty, 'How about a drink?'

'The Coonawarra is a fair drop,' Iain said. 'Strong finish …'

'Ta, muchly,' Mack said, using the phrase — an old favourite of Iain's — in parody of his friend's ritual wine talk. He squinted at the tie, wondering if there was a message in the hand-painted code.

The conversation returned to earlier topics. Arriving late, Mack found it difficult to find the rhythm; the jokes and references were largely dependant on what had gone before. He remained on the edge of things.

Iain was coming in for some playful teasing about his decision to send his son to a nearby private school.

'Mary's idea,' he protested.

'They offered Benjy a scholarship,' she hastened to explain. 'And it *is* the nearest school. Otherwise he'd be at a State school. Of course.'

More discussion followed, of little interest to Mack. He drained his wine, and transferred the cold, greasy sausages to the griddle of the nearby barbecue. High-tech, like most of Iain's possessions, the barbecue looked like a spin-off from a space programme: a moon-landing craft on a tripod. A handful of coals still glowed in the base; the remains of the crew perhaps, baked as their saucer re-entered earth's atmosphere too quickly, or at the wrong angle. The beers at the Club had loosened Mack's mind and he entertained himself with such thoughts, freely associating, as he shoved the sausages back and forth across the griddle with a pair of tongs. He drained another glass of wine, then ate the lukewarm sausages, wrapped in bread.

'I won't be sending my kids to a private school,' he announced, apropos of nothing except a dimly remembered conversation some minutes back.

Lisa was on her feet, holding a couple of empty salad bowls.

'You haven't *got* any kids,' she reminded him, and walked away towards the house, ostensibly carrying in the bowls, but with Anthea rising and following close on her heels, looking concerned.

'Coffee anyone?' Iain broke the embarrassed silence that followed. 'Mack?'

'Perhaps it's time to go,' he said, aware, dully, of some transgression.

'You just *got* here. You can't leave before the formalities.'

Iain lifted a small gift-wrapped parcel from a nearby table. 'We've all chipped in, Mack. A little … memento.'

'Not yet,' Mary told her husband. 'We've got to do this properly. Lisa should be here.'

She hurried into the house, reappearing shortly with Lisa in tow. Anthea failed to re-emerge. Iain waited until the circle of friends was attentive, and all murmuring had died away.

'Unaccustomed as I am …'

The subject was Mack, his life and times — but even the subject found it dull. His attention was wandering. He felt himself swaying, giddily; he caught Lisa's warning glare and made an extreme effort to remain stable, widening his stance. Concentrating on keeping himself upright, focused on each separate muscle, he missed his cue. Iain was offering the farewell gift into empty space, the smattering of polite applause had died away.

Something was expected of him. He reached out and accepted the gift, then stuffed it with difficulty into his pocket.

'Thanks. I'll add it to the collection.'

Puzzled amusement on several faces. 'You aren't going to open it?'

'Seen one, seen them all.'

Several guests giggled nervously. They hadn't a clue what their donation had bought.

'Ignore him,' Lisa hissed. 'Attention is what he wants.'

Her warning went unheeded; someone was curious enough to ask.

'Seen what?'

'Coffee mugs with cute little mottoes.'

More glances were exchanged, mostly in the direction of Iain. Surely not? The package was the wrong shape.

'Just teasing,' Mack said, and extracted the gift from his pocket and began fumbling with the crepe wrapping.

Iain said, 'Here, let me do that. You're handicapped.'

'I can manage.'

He unveiled, after further difficulties, a pen-case, covered with black felt, like a pelt of fine fur, as if to keep the pen warm.

'A black box,' he said. 'Just what I wanted.'

'Open it, smart arse.'

He held the gold pen, engraved with his name, aloft to a flourish of ironic applause.

'Speech,' someone said. A woman's voice: Anthea's, returned from the house, giving him rope. Giving him a *noose.* He grinned at her, responding, as always, to her challenge.

'It's a bit like sex,' he began.

'What is?'

Puzzled glances among the audience; rolled eyes of exasperation from Lisa.

He swayed, unsteadily. 'Out on the field. There's a special freedom — like sex. You're free of yourself. Almost ... unconscious.'

His speech was slurred, but still within the bounds of comprehension. The context, not the meaning, was proving difficult for his audience to grasp. What's-that-got-to-do-with-anything glances were sliding around the perimeter of faces.

'Unconscious is something you would know about,' Lisa muttered.

'This is my party,' he said. 'My speech. The rules are — you have to listen.'

He smiled beatifically; she averted her head in disgust.

'I'm trying to explain something. I'm trying to explain why I need to get away from school.'

'Because it's not like sex,' Anthea said. 'I think I get it.'

He turned to her, drunkenly, but with grudging respect, and waggled his finger.

'I don't think you *do* get it. Or not enough of it.'

A few sniggers rippled about the circle, but rebounded off Mack, leaving him untouched. The occasion, and the growing power of the wine had rendered him sentimental, and nostalgic. It had happened without warning, a switch flipping somewhere inside his head, an exact limit of blood alcohol reached and crossed.

'When I was a boy,' he said, 'it was like church. Saturday church.'

'What was?' Iain said, smirking. 'Sex?'

Mack pressed on, concentrating too much on getting his own thoughts and words out order to notice those of others.

'It was a ritual. Cleaning the boots, rubbing on the liniment. That was our — what's the word? — incense. And the smell of sweat …'

'It's time to go, Mack,' Lisa said.

'When I've finished. *You* especially have to listen.'

Anthea was shaking her head, enjoying the spectacle.

'I want to have my say,' he said. 'I've got important things to say.'

'You're pissed, Paul. You're talking in your sleep.'

The last phrase jolted him momentarily — but thinking it through seemed too hard.

'It's my party,' he said, 'and I'll get pissed if I want to.'

In fact he was only half-pissed; the booze had loosened his tongue, but not yet clouded his mind. Or clouded only the parts that needed clouding: the perception of his immediate surrounds, making room for other, older perceptions to emerge. Was he in fact talking in his sleep? He drained another glass of wine. He felt a rush of eloquence — his thoughts sounded eloquent from his side at least, from the inside. What emerged through the blender of mouth and tongue was another matter.

'It was a kind of magic,' he said, or thought he said. 'A kind of superstition …'

He was losing his audience. Iain was uncorking another bottle, Mary packing a basket with salad bowls and implements. Anthea's gold clasps and bracelets jangled softly somewhere.

He picked up a spoon and chimed it loudly against a wine glass.

'It's only a short speech,' he announced. 'Believe me it's much easier to listen to, than to give.'

Iain set down the bottle; Mary looked up, chastened. All eyes were on him, but distracted again by the present, by the here-and-now, he had lost his thread.

'We're waiting, Mack.'

Help from Mary: 'You were saying — you were superstitious.'

'Yeah. If my team won, I wrote down everything I'd done that morning before the game. Every little thing, no matter how stupid. Then I'd repeat the sequence the next Saturday — exactly. Get up at the same time, pull on my clothes in the same sequence. I used to iron my fucking *boot*-laces …'

That got their attention; even Lisa was watching, listening. He could only hope they were hearing the same words he was speaking.

'I used to unthread the laces after every game, wash them by hand, and iron them flat. I used to count my cornflakes into the bowl, flake by fucking flake. The same lucky number as the week before ...'

An opening for Anthea: 'You still remember the number?'

He turned to her, drunkenly grateful; his one true friend among the audience. 'Two hundred and fifty-three. How could I forget? I kept it up for months — till we lost a game.'

'What went wrong?'

'I played fucking badly.'

The two were cause and effect in those golden days.

Iain, still literal-minded, pressed him. 'But *why* did you play badly?'

'Maybe I counted wrong. Missed a cornflake.'

Iain laughed, and behind him, more importantly, a half-smile flickered on Lisa's face. A quarter-smile. At that moment it seemed to Mack, lost in his booze-rhapsody, that this was the nearest she had ever come to some kind of understanding of how much it meant to him.

Even Anthea was smiling. He was warming to her, more and more. A magical thinker herself, a believer in horoscopes, tarot cards, and dream messages, perhaps she could sympathise.

'I was the same on race day,' he said. 'My job was to

take the pigeons to the railway station, and check them in ...'

This was too dislocating; puzzled glances all around.

'You used to race pigeons?' Anthea asked.

'My *father* used to race pigeons,' he explained, patiently. Why didn't she know this? Surely everyone knew. 'But he was glued to his fucking armchair. It was my job to take them up, get them ringed. And get the clock set. He sat in the backyard waiting for them, scratching his back. He had this little ivory doo-wicky, hand-carved ...'

Lisa interrupted: 'What's this got to do with anything?'

Mack screwed up his eyes, concentrating hard, having trouble remembering what he meant himself. 'It's got to do with *every*thing,' he finally said. 'I was the same with the pigeons. I counted their seeds the same way. Handed them across the counter on race day in the same order. First the blues, then the pieds, then the grizzles. The cocks before the hens. Always ...'

He might have been speaking a foreign language, but his dear, wonderful friends were watching him, smiling and nodding. Their eyes seemed filled with tears of love and affection; or were the tears in his own eyes?

'I did the calling in each night the same way. Always held the tidbit in my left hand. Always stood exactly three paces from the landing board on the loft ...'

The realisation that they were smiling *at* him — at his crazy eloquence, his drunken sentimentality — and not with him, *simpatia*, only came later, on the way home.

Lisa was driving the milk truck, her car left behind at Anthea's. He was trying to tell her more; of walking home backwards from the Club after games, partly through superstition, partly not wanting to take his eyes from his second home. Of old Beppe and the superstitious routine he used every Saturday when he marked out the pitch. The booze was wearing off, but still Mack babbled on, drunk on memories.

'He grabbed back the spreader and actually crossed himself — I kid you not, he *crossed* himself, Lise — and with the sole of his fucking boot, the Catanzaro of his fucking boot, scrubbed out the lime …'

His right hand was resting lightly on her thigh; on Tuscany. Fuddled by booze and love, he mistook the shifting movements of her legs on the clutch and brake pedals for signs of sexual arousal. Aroused himself by those sliding thighs, he moved his hand upwards — the direction of Liguria, and the pleasures of the Riviera.

'Did I ever tell you about Beppe's Anatomy of the Leg?'

'A thousand times,' she said, and picked up his hand and threw it with force back into his own lap. This time he could see the tears in her eyes, definitely. What did they mean, he wondered, drunkenly? Rain in Lombardy? No — further north. In another country altogether.

'Speech Night is over,' she said. 'Will you please, *please* shut up?'

Spring

1

Day One of Mack's new life passed uneventfully. Woken by radio alarm at three a.m., he was queuing at the Mile End Depot at three-thirty. Within minutes, the tray was loaded; then came the steady routines of the work itself, the stop–start–stop of the truck, the padding through dark, silent streets and creaking gates and across crunching gravel or dew-slippery lawn.

The fibreglass cast offered little hindrance; he was able to flex his fingers sufficiently to grasp a carton, and even to pincer small change from doorsteps between thumb and forefinger. He soon learnt to savour the solitude and quiet, and the trance of the easy muscular rhythms. Lisa had sulked through the weekend, refusing to speak; he dreaded the end of the day, and what it might hold. But for these hours he need think no further than the next gate or pile of coins.

Of course the boy, Shaun, wasn't waiting. Mack drove slowly past his house, hand-braked the truck, and walked quietly back to deposit two cartons of milk on the doorstep. Was he in there? Tucked safely in bed, with a mug of hot milk and a teddy bear? Or was he riding the trains, with a shoulder bag full of clinking cans of spraypaint?

Mack was home by eight, but the house was empty; Lisa had left for work. The last in a long series of scribbled notes that had marked his round, like clues in a treasure hunt leading him from house to house, was clamped to the fridge door by a magnet in the shape of a brightly-coloured parrot.

BACK LATE. CURRY IN FRIDGE.

At least she was speaking again, if only by fridge-gram. He slept through the morning, rose at noon, showered, and caught the weepy end of a midday movie over a bowl of cereal. A housework roster had been drawn up, part of the final negotiations with Lisa. He attended to Monday's requirement — bathroom cleaning — then spent time with his weights: mostly biceps curls with his free arm, and some leg work.

Vince dropped in at two, laden with foil cartons of Chinese take-away and two six-pack slabs of light beer. This last annoyed Mack; the choice seemed patronising, or worse, a message.

'Where's the missus, Mack?'

'Work.'

Clearly disappointed, Vince did his best to hide it. 'All the more for us.'

Mack carried bowls and serving spoons out onto the terrace, Vince following with the beer and food.

Conversation over lunch proved difficult; a new awkwardness seemed to have arisen between them. Vince was interested in news of the milk round — gross takings, delivery times, litreage — but sidestepped any questions about the Club. Instead, they occupied their mouths with the clumsy rituals of eating with chopsticks, exaggerating the mechanical problems at times to avoid having to speak.

'So how's business?' Mack asked.

'So-so. Bit of a slump.'

'Nothing much happening around here.'

Vince looked out over the timber rib cages of the surrounding houses, the pallets of bricks waiting to be laid, and shook his head, sadly. 'Aldo bit off more than he could chew.'

'You in trouble?'

'Nothing we can't handle.'

'You want to save some money? Sack Colby. I'll do the job for free.'

Vince ignored the advice. 'Heard from Bruno?'

'One postcard. Leaning Tower of Pisa. Reckons he had to drive into Switzerland to post it. Doesn't trust the Italian postal system.'

Vince laughed. 'Where is he?'

Mack tapped his groin. 'Torino. Got a trial with a couple of clubs.'

'Juventus?' asked Vince, not seriously.

233

'In his dreams. Couple of third division clubs.'

'So you might have the milk round forever?'

'I've got a feeling he'll be back sooner than he thinks.'

In the late afternoon they drove in separate cars to the Norwood squash courts, and here, in the white-walled pit, words were not required at all, or only a ritual exchange of exclamations and monosyllables within the more powerful, physical conversation of the game. *Fault! Let! Shot!*

Home at six, Mack heated the curry, and ate while watching television, tracking two movies with frequent channel changes before settling on the Monday night football. He had played the game at school as a boy, real football, Australian football. The sport still spoke to him. He had loved its random, slapstick quality, especially in the winter mud: the unpredictable bounce of the slippery, suppository-shaped ball. More greased pig than dog, it obeyed no known law of motion, refusing to sit, heel, chase.

In the end he had chosen the round ball, chosen to play 'the foot', *il calcio*, instead of playing footy. The reason, he liked to joke: it was handy. He had chosen wogball — his father's word — because, simply, it was there, just across the road. Not that his father had much cared, either way. He despised the immigrant code when he remembered to notice it, 'a girl's game', but the man's game was also beneath him. His only sport was his pigeons.

Mack peeled off his clothes and fell across the bed at eleven. Heavy rain woke him at two, an hour earlier than the radio alarm. Lisa's body was now beside him, sleeping. The sound of water gurgling in the gutters and downpipes seemed to fill his bladder also; after rising and emptying himself, he stood for some time at the door, listening.

'Open the door a little,' Lisa called from the bed, muffled. 'I like to hear it.'

'Sorry. Didn't mean to wake you.' He slid the door open, a hand's breadth. 'How was the book club?'

'You should come and find out. What time is it?'

Four luminous red digits floated, disembodied, in a corner of the dark room.

'Bit past two.'

'What time are you off?'

'Might wait a bit. See if the rain settles.'

He sensed her prop herself on an elbow; heard the sip taken from the glass of water she kept by her bed.

'Anthea is having a barbecue next Saturday,' she said. 'Did I tell you?'

'You know Saturdays are difficult for me.'

'Come late. It's fine. You're not the guest of honour this time.'

Her voice, blurred with sleep, half-obscured by the

noise of the rain outside, sounded warm and forgiving. If he concentrated hard enough, perhaps he might hear the actual sound of her smile: the noise of lips parting, stretching.

'They're your friends. You go. You don't need me there. I'll drop in after the shop-talk for a drink.'

'Please come,' she said. 'There's a couple I want you to meet. The Prices. Friends of Anthea's.'

'Anthea has friends?'

'Can you stop joking long enough to listen, Mack? They've just adopted a baby from Korea.'

He shivered, goose-pimpling. The cold air streaming steadily through the narrow door crack had washed the last bed-warmth from his skin. He slid the door shut and climbed back into bed; they snuggled together, a good fit, as always. Boxed cutlery.

'You're freezing.'

He wasn't listening, her previous words still occupied his mind. 'You're considering adopting?'

'It's an option.' She paused before continuing. 'I know you don't want children. What I'm afraid is — what if we regret it later? When it's too late?'

'I don't see any point in what-ifs. You have to make decisions on how you feel *now*.'

Her fingers strayed towards his groin, tangling themselves in the tough, springy pubic wool. But the discussion had depressed him; the sexual act was once

236

again contaminated by matters which had nothing to do with simple need, or pleasure. The waking stiffness that had vanished when he rose to urinate would not return.

'I think the rain is easing,' he said. 'Maybe I'll get an early start.'

He freed himself from the gentle clasp of her body, and rolled out from beneath the quilt. Then he sat on the edge of the bed, and turned back to face her general direction somewhere in the darkness.

'It's not necessarily that I don't want children, Lise. If you want them, of course I want them. But it's a big expense. Maybe when we get our own place.'

'When will that be on a milkman's wages? We've got no money, Mack.'

'Is that my fault? You wanted to go overseas too.'

It seemed an important point to make. Their savings had been spent, in part, on her convalescence.

He pressed on. 'It would be tough on a kid at present. It's hard when you can't have things you want, the things that other kids have. You might not know it, but I do.'

In the darkness the bedsheets rustled, restlessly. 'Not the wrong-side-of-the-tracks routine again.'

He was immediately enraged. 'You wouldn't *know* about it! Did your father trash the house every month? Beat your mother senseless?'

'I wasn't so lucky.'

237

'What the fuck do you mean by that?'

She seemed to sense that some chalk-line had been crossed, and checked herself.

'Okay. I'm sorry. I meant nothing by it.'

'No, tell me what you meant.'

Another pause, as if she was deciding. 'You do make a meal of all that stuff! It's so *important* to you. For God's sake — he was nothing like that.'

'Not when you knew him, maybe. Once I got too big to push around he quietened down.'

Once had been all that was needed. Mack had heard the pension night argument as he crossed the road after training: his father blaming his mother for some misdemeanour, or agreeing with her self-blame. Only his voice had been raised that night, not his fists — but Mack, toughened by a season in the first team, had been waiting for an excuse. Years of rage at last found an expression, or outlet; even now, he shivered thinking about the damage he had done.

'After I beat the shit out of him he never touched her again.'

'Very noble,' Lisa said. 'But you left out one detail. Last time you told me the story you said you did it for you, not for her.'

Mack paused before speaking again, thinking.

'Maybe. Whatever — I put the bastard in hospital, and I'm still glad.'

238

'Then you're just the same as him. Two drops of water, is that the phrase?'

'There's a difference. I wasn't drunk. I knew exactly what I was doing.'

'Then you're even *worse* than him.'

He wasn't listening as he pulled on his work clothes. His mind was elsewhere, feeling its way like a tongue around the edges of the tender spot, the wound which she had located, almost accidentally.

'I did him a favour,' he eventually said. 'He was always trying to fake his way into hospital. I gave him a reason.'

'The man I knew had plenty of reasons. He was just a helpless old pensioner.'

'He *deserved* his illnesses.'

'He deserved to die?'

The bluntness of the question stopped Mack dead. He felt cornered, and still angry.

'He talked himself into dying,' he finally told her. 'He pointed the bone at himself. All those tribunals and medical reports and bullshit illnesses …'

He walked out of the room before she could argue further, but she wasn't so easily dismissed. She jumped up out of the bed and followed, shouting after him.

'But he didn't die, did he? He lives on — that's the real joke!'

Her last words stayed with him throughout the

239

round, interrupting the trance of work, the mindlessness which he had prized the previous morning. Only when Mack was home again, in bed in an empty house, sleeping through the balance of the morning, could he find some escape from her accusation, and from the anger it had kindled.

2

He was early again at the Club that night, keen to get out on the park and lose his troubles in exhaustion, or at least deprive his brain of the energy needed to worry about those troubles.

Colby was waiting at the entrance to the players' race, clipboard in hand.

'I'd like a word, Mack.'

'Now?'

Intentionally or not, the coach stood in a manner that barred passage.

'Now.'

'Where?'

His gaze took in Mack's sprigged boots; inside was out of question.

'Maybe out on the field.'

He moved aside, and followed Mack up the race, onto the grass. The rest of the players were still in the change rooms, the stand empty of members.

'I won't beat about the bush, Mack. I've got a new player coming over. Scotty McNab from Hellenic.'

'Good player. Not much finesse — but solid.'

Colby shrugged. 'The squad is too big. Someone has to be disappointed.'

'You want my advice on who to drop?'

Colby grimaced, rodent-toothed. 'This is hard. I know you've given great service to the Club.'

The idea of being cut was so distant from Mack's mind, so absurd, that even as Colby spoke the words, they didn't penetrate.

'Your style of play doesn't fit in with mine.'

Slowly, ponderously, he saw the obvious. 'Me? You want to cut *me?*'

The coach stared at him, unfazed.

'I'm the best you've *got.*'

'On your day you're a quality player,' Colby conceded.

'That's very fucking generous of you.'

'That's the other problem.'

'What?'

'The mouth. The sarcasm. You've always got to have the last word. Your little private joke.'

'Helps grease the wheels, I always thought.'

Colby shook his head. 'It's an attitude problem, Mack. Then there are the injuries.' He gestured towards the foam-padded cast. 'How many games you play last season? You've already missed six this year.'

'You think I *want* the injuries?'

For the first time Colby averted his eyes.

'You do! I'm right, aren't I? You think I go around shooting myself in the fucking foot!'

The coach stared back at him, this time unwavering. 'Then there's your attitude to training. You wander off whenever you like …'

'Christ, what planet are you from? Look around — I'm the first one here!'

'It's more than that. It's a sign. You don't fit in. You're a … disruptive influence.' The schoolteacher's pat phrase sat oddly in Colby's mouth; he paused, as if surprising himself by the sound of it. 'You're never part of the team — always on the edge of things, passing some smart remark.'

'You don't want a happy team?'

The volume of their voices, barely civil, had risen enough to stop all movement in the change rooms behind Mack. A head turtled around the door then was withdrawn, remaining inside, pretending not to listen.

'I don't give a fuck whether the lads are happy or sad — as long as they play the game *my* way.'

'I don't believe this.'

'It happens to all of us,' Colby said, and for the first time there was something softer in his hard, high voice. 'It has to be faced, son. I don't believe in pulling punches.'

Mack looked away from him, across the green turf.

Colby said, 'This is difficult for me.'

Mack laughed, harshly. 'Bullshit. You're loving it.'

'You're not making it easy.'

One trump remained for Mack, one last *trionfo*, a word shouted every few minutes across the table tops inside the Club.

'The committee's not going to like it. No way. You haven't a snowball's chance in hell. I've got a lot of friends in the Club.'

Their eyes met; Colby's answer seemed reluctant. 'You think so? Look around. Where are all your dago friends?'

Mack realised, suddenly, that none of the committee were in the Club rooms. Vince, Aldo: not a single Club official had been sighted since he arrived for training. The bar was empty.

'You need me,' he said.

'I need no *one*,' Colby said, with an emphatic second syllable. 'I need a team.'

'Bruno is gone. You're going to lose your two most experienced players in one week?'

'You're not a defender, son. You said so yourself. You can't fill his boots.'

The two men stood watching each other. Mack's fists were tightly clenched, he might have been a boxer, waiting for an opening.

'The game is changing,' Colby went on. 'System. Science. The days of the maverick are over.'

'Says you.'

'Says the facts. If you're not joking out there with the lads, you're thinking. I don't know which is worse. You're always giving orders, switching game-plans. The players listen too much to you. You *think* too much. I don't want players who think; *I'm* paid to do the bleedin' thinking.'

'You could have said before. I'll try and keep my mouth shut.'

The words leaked out, or were bleated out, before he had time to think them through; he immediately regretted the plaintive tone.

Colby relaxed, his sharp features softening. He had won, and knew it; but there was no triumph in the expression. He seemed genuinely sad.

'I'm sorry, Mack. I don't think you can help it. I admire your skills. Like I said — quality. On your day. And I've often laughed with your jokes. But I can't use them here. Get your knee right and you might have a few more years. Plenty of clubs will be interested.'

'Maybe. Or maybe I'll stay. There's an old saying around here: *un pranzo comprende molte pietanze.*'

'I'll let you play your little game. What's it mean?'

Many dishes make a meal? More than that. You've won the battle but not the war? It was less the content of the phrase than the language that made the intended point: that Colby was still a foreigner, an outsider. That

245

he had as little understanding of the inner workings of the Club as he had of that one simple phrase.

'It means I've seen coaches come and go. I've got a feeling I might outlast you yet.'

At this Colby snorted, shook his head and turned and walked away towards the race. Then he stopped, and turned back, but still speaking without anger, clearly and patiently.

'You think you speak the lingo around here, Mack? If you do, you're not listening. You don't know a thing — not a bleedin' thing. They're selling you down the river.'

'They want me in the team,' Mack said. 'It's something you wouldn't know much about. We go a long way back. We're … family.'

There was no anger in Colby's expression, but there was something else. As the coach spoke again Mack glimpsed it for the first time: pity.

'Sure they did their best. Aldo twisted my arm. He wanted you in the team — but not for the reasons you think. You're naive, son. You need to grow up.'

'What the fuck are you talking about?'

'Ask them. Ask your precious dago family. If you can find them.'

Mack shivered, a sudden, claustrophobic chill. All the *trionfi* were in Colby's hands; he clearly knew something.

'Tell me what you *mean*, fuck you!'

'One thing I will tell you: I won't be having you back. Unless half a dozen players break their legs. But it's nothing personal — and you can believe that or not. I don't give a stuff.'

One committee member, Gino Trimboli, was waiting in the change rooms, signs of eavesdropping written clearly on his face.

'Shit — I'm sorry, Mack. I had no idea. No one tells me anything.'

'Someone knew. The Club rooms are fucking empty!'

Gino uttered the usual placating noises. 'Maybe it's for the best. A good rest will help the knee.' A pause, and a tentative grin: 'Rome's still a bit swollen. You can get stuck into the exercises ...'

'Fuck off.'

Mack ripped the foam padding from his wrist, pulled on his jeans and sandshoes, and entered the Club rooms. One or two juniors were hanging about, their dads engrossed in Broom. No other committee members were in sight. Mack tapped himself a beer, gulped it down, then drank several more in quick succession. He filled a jug and carried it outside, finding a seat high in the stand.

The players were grouped in fours, sprinting ten metres, turn and back, ten metres, turn and back: fitness training. He felt a huge welling of frustration and anger inside him, a rapidly rising gorge that seemed to fill his chest.

'Bring out the balls,' he yelled. 'It's supposed to be a ball game! Where are the balls?'

'Ignore him, lads,' Colby told the distracted players. 'He's entitled to let off steam.'

The handful of members who were now watching the training glanced towards Mack, and moved a few paces away, dissociating themselves. The pressure continued to mount inside Mack, choking his throat, spreading into his limbs. He stood abruptly, and drunkenly hurled the heavy glass beer jug far out among the players.

'You fucking ferret! I can run rings around you and you know it.'

Colby calmly bent and picked up the jug, miraculously unshattered. He walked towards the stand, and set it down, gently, on the bench beside Mack.

'You want the truth, I'll give you the truth,' he said, quietly.

Something in his lowered voice also quietened Mack. He waited, apprehensive, and aware of a further humiliation. He was no longer a threat, no anger needed to be wasted on him.

'Your little mate Aldo is broke. That's the truth. The Club's got no money. They can't afford promotion.'

Still Mack didn't see it; Colby continued talking as if to a six year old, joining the dots.

'Looked at the premiership table lately? We're top, three points clear. Heading for the First Division. It's an expensive business, winning.'

As he uttered these last words, the facts clarified, abruptly, for the first time.

'Aldo wanted me in the team to *lose!*' Mack said, stunned.

Colby's small jockey's face remained impassive. 'It took me a while to twig, too.'

'They thought I was a fucking *liability!* A handicap!'

His thoughts were in turmoil; he knew instantly it was the truth, it had the simple logic, the sheer explaining power, of the truth. He rose, agitated, shifting restlessly from foot to foot.

'You *were* carrying injuries,' Colby said, another rare thoughtfulness.

Mack turned his head and walked away, wanting to distance himself as far as possible from Colby's pity. But more words of crude sympathy followed him up the race, licking at him with rough kindness, like the tongue of a dog.

'I'm sorry it had to be me, McNeil. Like I say, I've nothing personal. You were a quality player. But I've got a championship to win.' The words were uttered matter-of-factly; then his voice hardened again. 'I'm going to

249

shove promotion so far up this bleedin' dago committee it'll cost them every stick of spaghetti they've got. You want to blame someone, *they're* the villains.'

3

'I've invited some people over on Sunday.'

Home late from work, Lisa had found Mack, three-quarters drunk, sitting on the terrace, staring out over the city.

'I met them at Anthea's,' she said. 'The Prices. Did I mention them before?'

Engrossed in his own troubles, he took some time to listen to what she was saying, to hear the words. When he did, her disingenuousness infuriated him; did she think she could slip the name under his guard, as if for the first time?

'Let me guess — the Korean baby, right?'

Something in his tone, or perhaps the row of crushed, empty beer cans on the barbecue table, warned her to tread carefully. She sought escape in neutral topics.

'What's for dinner?'

'I wasn't hungry,' he said.

Her mouth opened, provoked — then closed again, swallowing the obvious answer before it was uttered.

He spoke the words for her. 'If *you're* hungry, I'll make some pasta.'

'I'll do it,' she said, abruptly, and turned back inside the house.

He turned his gaze again to the west, to the vast dome of empty air above the city, a nothingness his eyes could lose themselves in, unfocused. The sun was long gone, the sky had deepened from blue to indigo. The brilliant incandescence of the flood lights of the Club, far to the west, demanded focus, drew his eyes to them. He screwed his eyes shut. The world shrank within earshot: a sound-horizon of rumbling traffic, the occasional dog bark or high-pitched child's shout drifting up from the leafy suburbs below. But the Club would not be shut out, the after-glow of those flood lights seemed seared into his lids.

He opened his eyes, but averted his head, and stood and entered the house without looking back. Dinner — spaghetti sauce emptied from a jar — was bubbling thickly on the gas-range inside.

'So you want to buy a baby from Korea?'

She stirred the contents of the saucepan, without answering.

'I think we should talk about it,' he said.

'This isn't the time, Paul.'

'Why not?'

'Because you're spoiling for a fight.'

'No, tell me,' he said. 'Why do you suddenly want to adopt? We haven't even got my test back yet.'

'You're drunk.'

'Only a little. It helps me think.'

He watched her dislodge a frosted parcel of ravioli from the freezer compartment, thump it twice against the bench, and shake the frozen contents into the boiling water, engrossing herself in the act.

'I think I'll ring him,' he said.

'Who?'

'The family medicine man.'

'It's after six. No one will be there.'

'You never know.'

The doctor's card — a flat magnetic rectangle — was stuck to the fridge door, among the coloured fruits and flowers and parrots. He reached for the wall-phone and dialled. A receptionist's smooth voice answered. He asked to be put through to 'Bill', hoping that a little first-name familiarity might open some doors.

'Whom shall I say is calling?'

'Paul McNeil.'

Lisa stirred the simmering ravioli as background muzak played softly in his ear: aquarium music, interrupted after a time by an equally soothing male voice.

'Mr McNeil? What can I do for you?'

'About my test result. Is it back?'

A short hesitation. Had the doctor forgotten already?

'Yes, it is. It might be best if you made an appointment. These things are difficult on the phone.'

'It's simple, surely. A number. Black and white.'

'It's more a shade of grey, I'm afraid.'

Mack stood with the phone pressed to the side of his head, a little giddy with booze, trying to make sense of what he was hearing. His output — his words, his energy — seemed heightened, if anything, by alcohol. The input was restricted, dulled, difficult to decipher.

'A low count is not the end of the world. Further tests are needed to clarify ...'

'The count is low?'

The old, experienced voice continued. 'I'd prefer to talk with you face to face.'

'I'd prefer to talk about it *now*. What are you trying to tell me? No tadpoles?'

His pulse was racing, all his senses suddenly alert. Everything around him seemed significant. Lisa slid off her stool and moved out of his peripheral vision; he turned to find her slumped on the sofa, staring out the front window across the city.

'Ah — I wouldn't put it like that. Some tadpoles. But perhaps not quite enough.'

A sudden piercing thought, a headlight through the fog. 'What about the miscarriage?'

Mack's words were aimed not so much into the phone as at his wife, on the other side of the room.

He said, 'You know she had a miscarriage a few years back.'

The phone remained utterly silent, the sound of embarrassment.

'She got pregnant a couple of years ago,' he repeated. 'How the fuck do you explain that?'

The voice finally found an answer. 'Perhaps your — ah — sub-fertility is a recent thing. Have you had some kind of viral infection in the last few years?'

'What kind of virus?'

'Mumps, for instance.'

Mack hung up the receiver, walked across the room and sat in the armchair opposite his wife. He felt suddenly completely sober. For a time neither spoke.

'There must be some mistake,' she hoped.

'You made the mistake. Letting me have the test.'

'I didn't even think … Not for one moment. It was just a formality.'

His mind was a whirling food-blender, a mix of urgent feelings jostling for precedence.

'Christ! Whose child *was* it?'

She couldn't answer, or even meet his eyes.

'Tell me, fuck you!'

'It was only once!' she finally blurted out, towards the window. 'I was *sure* it was ours.'

'Great.'

'You're no saint,' she said. 'What about that porn

night? You were out all night …'

'You *know* I was delivering milk.'

'And the hospital,' she said. 'No one would talk to you. The nurses wouldn't go *near* you. You must have been up to something!'

'If you think that, you don't know me at all.'

He rose and jerked open the sliding door forcefully, dislocating it from its groove, and stepped outside. Lisa followed, but no further than the doorway, standing in the frame, neither inside nor out.

When she spoke it was towards the city, still unable to face him. 'I might go and stay at Anthea's for a few days.'

'Why go there?' he said. 'Have you been fucking her, too?'

He could say whatever he pleased, whatever he thought, however unforgivable. The lights of the distant Club had faded, training must be over — the perception, and the conclusion, came to him clearly, as if part of his mind was seeking distraction, trying to find something else to think about.

'You don't want to clear up this little mystery before you go?'

'I'm not ready to talk about it, Mack. I simply *can't*. I didn't think it would come to this. Okay?'

She turned back inside, towards the bedroom. After a few minutes he followed her. Her suitcase was open on the bed, a yawning hippo mouth into which clothes were being thrown. He jerked open the top drawer in her chest and began to toss her clothes himself, with his free hand, the counterweight of his heavy cast swinging furiously back and forth at his side.

'At least it wasn't the milkman,' he said. 'I can personally testify that you haven't been fucking the milkman!'

She jammed the lid shut. 'If it makes any difference — I'm sorry. It was a one-off thing. A curriculum conference.'

'You mean it's someone I *know*?'

'It's not important who it was. It meant nothing. I'd had too much to drink.' She turned to him, her first show of defiance. 'Surely *you* can understand that …'

And then he remembered: a long-distance phone call at seven one Sunday morning, from the conference centre, her voice, hoarse, weary, sentimental, waking him to tell him how much she was missing him.

He had heard the false note then, but ignored it: the voice of too much protest.

'I was a different person,' she said, pleading. 'It wasn't *me*.'

His arm — the arm encased in fibreglass — seemed to lift itself. She stood her ground, staring him in the eyes, calmly, waiting, as if willing it herself. Her look killed some of the rage in him, but the movement of the arm was autonomous, even necessary. The cast seemed to render that arm the property of someone else, as if its inanimate bulk, not part of his flesh, was under other control. He struck her once across the cheek, holding back at the last moment, but brutally enough to snap her head to one side. She screwed her eyes shut, and bit her lip, but didn't cry out. There was something ritual in her acceptance of the blow.

His heavy arm dropped back to his side. He stood watching her, regretting the violence instantly.

'I'm sorry.'

It wasn't *me*, he almost told her, but immediately suppressed the stupid words. Enough damage had been done. Her high cheek-bone was grazed: redness was already seeping from the abraded skin. He could see that she was in pain. She clasped shut the lid of her suitcase.

'I'll carry it for you,' he offered, absurdly.

'Thanks.'

He lifted the suitcase from the bed with his good arm and followed her out the front door, and down the marble steps to her car. The scene still had the unreality of something he was outside of, watching: a drama of beaten wives and packed suitcases. The Display Home had the feel of a television set, a Californian façade of white columns and wide staircases.

'You okay?' he said.

She touched the tips of her fingers to the raw

abrasion on her cheek. The sight of her nails, bitten to the quick, seemed suddenly human, and poignant, and real. This was Lisa, his wife of fifteen years. It was Lisa he had struck.

'I'll mend.'

As she drove away he clung to the note of implicit forgiveness in her words, but perhaps that was wishful thinking. Wishful hearing. The reality of what he had done was beginning to dawn on him; he knew that he would never forgive himself.

4

He slept, dead-drunk, through the morning alarm. The grumble of diesel engines woke him mid-morning, too late to deliver milk. Milk was the last thing on his mind. He wandered out onto the terrace, naked, his eyes screwed shut against the glare of day. Two flat-top trucks were backing, with much gear-crunching, onto the neighbouring lots. Each carried a compact yellow forklift, piggyback; when the mother-truck had been properly positioned, the cub was unramped, and the stacks of bricks that had sat on their pallets for months began to be raised onto the trays.

Aldo's dream was folding. Mack stepped back inside the house, and riffled through the Yellow Pages. He rang the first listing under 'Locksmiths' that caught his eye, a 24-hour emergency line. After showering, he sat outside on the terrace, breakfasting on beer, waiting for the locksmith, reaching now and then for his binoculars. The world continued to disassemble itself about him. By early afternoon only the wooden rib cages of Tuscan Heights remained, isolated in their weedy lots. Would they too be reclaimed? The timber, split by summer heat and warped by autumn rain, was surely ruined beyond salvage, or receivership.

The locksmith arrived, an agile teenage prodigy wearing a Metallica T-shirt and a mobile phone in a holster. Mack drank on, steadily, as the locks were changed to the beat of a ghetto-blaster. The new, chunky deadlocks would keep out Aldo, or his bailiffs — but in his haste Mack had not foreseen the obvious: what if Lisa chose to return? How would she get in? Of course, if she *didn't* return, ever, it would solve the problem. Half-drunk, not wanting to think of anything beyond the simple mechanics of keys and locks, this seemed to him the simplest solution. Her absence, their separation, had suddenly contracted to a problem in logistics, easily managed. Somewhere to the west a huge, revolving cloud of birds caught his eye. He reached again for the binoculars, but found them of little use. Pigeons? Too large and too slow-moving. Parrots, perhaps. Cockatoos. He was still camped on the terrace, birdwatching, long after the trucks and the locksmith had left. The house was secure, at least temporarily, but felt claustrophobic when he ventured in for another six-pack: a prison of low ceilings and close walls. The dimensions of the outside world seemed only marginally greater, and shrinking fast. Lisa was gone, the neighbouring Dream Homes had been loaded onto the backs of trucks and taken away. What next?

The dismantling of hills and trees? The raising of sections of sky like vast blue-painted backdrops, leaving — what?

The flood lights of the Club remained in the far distance: four tiny vertical sticks of magnesium ribbon, glowing fiercely at the tip. He sat at the barbecue table, drinking steadily, wanting nothing more than to be between those light towers, a ball snuffling loyally at his feet. At eight sharp the flare of the lights also faded, abruptly. He was left with the disconnected glitter of the city below, and the night sky above, a patchwork of cloud and star. An odd, drunken perception: he was possibly closer to deep space, a few miles above his head, than he was to the western suburbs of Adelaide. And he was probably closer to the molten core of the planet, a few miles beneath his feet, than he was to the Club. He shivered, involuntarily, struck by a sense of precariousness, of the sheer thinness of the city spread before him, with its shallow smear of green.

Where did such weird thoughts come from? The row of cans on the table? When he had emptied the last of these, and crushed it in his fist, he located a cask of white wine in the back of the fridge, and broke open the cardboard container to milk the last drops from the silvered bladder.

Towards midnight even the lights of the city were taken from him. A wide rain front moved ponderously in from the gulf, a dark wave that was more an absence than a presence, swallowing the streetlights progressively as it rolled across the city towards the Hills. Soon he could hear it: whispering across the suburbs of the Volvo Belt below, then rushing up the hill, a sudden downpour that forced him inside. Trapped, he roamed the house restlessly. Anger, held in check by the alcohol, began to assert itself; he felt an urge to lash out at the ridiculous Dream Home, to kick at the polished teak doors and terrazzo floors and marble fittings. His fibreglass arm also irked him. A hindrance, certainly — but also a reminder. Among the graffiti of autographs and bawdy poems and felt-tip cartoons was a single brown stain of dried blood.

A pair of scissors were excavated from the kitchen oddments drawer and quickly blunted. Lisa's secateurs, in the gardening cupboard downstairs, were better suited to the job; he hacked at the cast for some time, managing to rip it free, in shreds.

The unencumbered wrist felt stiff, but also weightless, a lighter-than-air butterfly wing, floating upwards unless held firmly and deliberately to his side.

This, too, he managed to find annoying.

He wasn't hungry — food seemed irrelevant — but his restlessness propelled him as often into the kitchen as into every other room. Once there he gathered food automatically, as if grazing, from fridge and cupboard.

The act of eating proved helpful, more as a distraction than a consolation: occupational therapy for a mouth that wanted to shout not eat. Diverted by the movements of biting and chewing, the tight muscles of his face relaxed. A discovery: with the removal of this outward expression of anger and restlessness, he was also soothed at a deeper level, as if the expression of anger *was* the anger, or a greater part of it.

Food also acted as ballast. Slowed by the weight of a dozen slices of stale bread and whatever spreads came to hand, he sank into the sofa. Deprived of the diversion of anger, he was left again with his guilt. He channel-hopped till three a.m., then left for the Depot, more late-owl than early bird, motivated not so much by a responsibility to his clients as by the need to do something, to avoid thinking. He left the house open for Lisa. In case. The absurdity of those new locks, unused, struck him — but a visit from Aldo seemed unlikely between the hours of midnight and dawn. Rain was still falling, steadily. Encased in Bruno's plastic poncho and hood he jogged through the wet streets from doorstep to truck to doorstep. The slippery cartons felt like blocks of ice, and a deep, cold ache seeped up through the bones of his arms. The milk round had never seemed such a stupid idea. On every third or fourth doorstep an abusive note was weighted beneath coins. Rain had blurred much of the anger of the scrawling felt-tip letters; what remained was a variation on a single theme: NO MILK YESTERDAY. The accusation had an odd, alternate sense, shifting in and out of focus like an optical illusion, difficult to grasp, half non sequitur, half an order placed with a milkman travelling backwards in time. If only he could. His fingers were as numb as his mind; he fumbled the coins; several times he abandoned them where they fell. His legs seemed equally uncoordinated; mid-round he fell heavily on a slippery lawn, and from that point slowed his pace, limping, finishing later than usual.

Dawn brought an improvement in visibility, somehow a dull light squeezed around or through the roof of dark cloud. Sweating despite the cold, he tugged off the glistening poncho, tossed it into the tray of the truck among the empty crates, and sat exhausted on the bench in the cabin, windows wound down, allowing the air, cleaned by rain, to cool his face.

Regal Park Cemetery marked the terminus of the round; the gravestones were emerging from the darkness like the blurred faces of the dead themselves. A public phone box stood at the main entrance, half a block distant. Lit from within, it glowed, waveringly, through the distorting lens of the wet windscreen. An odd choice of location, Mack thought — closer to the dead than to the living. The usual jokes half-formed in his mind, but there were no ears to utter them into, or

265

none above ground. Two days had passed since his last human contact. Two nights, more accurately, but nights were now, in effect, his days. He had scribbled his signature on a Depot invoice poked at him from a teller's window by a disembodied hand, he had pieced together a hundred dissolving messages on doorsteps — these were the limits of his social life.

He flipped open the glove box, and tugged out the stash of dope in its sealed plastic bag. Using a dozen cigarette-papers in overlapping shingle fashion, he rolled himself a huge unwieldy joint, or toke. Were they still called tokes? It had been years since he had smoked. Blimp might have been a better description. A cannabis blimp, a cannabis zeppelin. He twisted both ends tightly, for structural reasons, bit one off, cigar-style, lit the other, and inhaled, deeply and steadily.

The first touch of the drug inside his head was pure nausea, followed immediately by dizziness; it took some minutes for this unwanted high to be subsumed by a dreamy, easeful clarity.

For the first time since bashing Lisa he felt at peace with the world, felt serene enough even to accept that word, bashing, into his mind as an accurate description. A single restlessness remained: he wanted to share that peace. He inhaled again, deeply, and stared about. He wanted to pass the smouldering parcel.

The glove box caught his eye; he reached in again

and fossicked, one-handed. The business card — stiff, sharp-cornered — wasn't difficult to find by touch. He climbed down from the cabin and walked to the phone box, some distance off. He might have driven the fifty yards, but the thought didn't enter his head. What was a little rain? *Was* it, in fact, still raining? If so, on whose head and face and shoulders? Someone who wore his clothes and his skin, it seemed, but was located at a further circumference of sensation. The inhaled vapour of his burning package, sheltered in the cup of both hands, warmed him from inside out, and also armoured him, rendering his senses magically invulnerable to the wet and the cold.

The embossed phone number looked upmarket, an eastern suburbs number, the very best of those suburbs no doubt, the kind of area that only criminals could now afford. He dialled; the phone rang repeatedly; a woman's voice finally answered, muzzy with sleep.

'Who is it?'

'Monique?'

'Who's this?'

'Mack.'

All the world knows Mack.

'I'm sorry — I'm half-asleep. Who did you say … ?'

'Mack. From the Club.'

'Last Saturday night?'

'A few months back. You danced for us.'

The superiority of weed over booze: it did not obstruct, or disable, the tongue. It had no effect on the machinery of speech at all. If anything, it eased the flow, each phrase emerging as if gift-wrapped in its own smoky talk-balloon.

'I dance at a lot of clubs. I gave you my card?'

'We had that drink afterwards. Remember?'

'Sort of, Mick.'

'Mack.'

'How are you, Mack?'

'Lonely. I wondered — I know it's late — maybe we could get together?'

'It's so late it's early, Mack. I'm in bed with my husband. I could see you later …'

Mack stood in the booth, the receiver pressed to one ear, Olympian in his patience. He rounded his lips and with a light push of his tongue released a smoke-ring into the world. An old skill, but never forgotten; it floated ponderously towards the door before unravelling, caught in the slipstream of the falling rain. The murmured voices at the far end of the phone — female, male — were barely audible. Then came the female again, loud in his ear.

'Could you ring back in the morning?'

'It *is* the morning.'

'It's the middle of the night, Mick.'

'I could come to your place. If you can't meet me at

the cemetery.'

This last phrase sounded hilarious. He guffawed, spluttering puffs of smoke, as if communicating by smoke signal instead of telephone. The sharp click at the other end of the phone was merely an excuse for more laughter. 'Meet me at the cemetery,' he crooned softly, to the melody of some unidentifiable tune.

Rain was still falling, but was now more of a drizzle. He stepped out of the luminous booth and walked through the cemetery gates, sucking at the remnants of his joint before casting it aside. The butt seemed to descend in slow motion, a burning Hindenburg, disintegrating into tiny embers, instantly quenched in the dark puddles. He walked on through the straight, narrow avenues and streets of the cemetery, surrounded by flat upright stones as if by a miniature Manhattan.

He remembered again that night in childhood when he had wandered these little streets under a full moon, wanting desperately to be spooked. Nothing had happened, and he had woken next morning in bland sunshine, and trudged home, disappointed.

From that time he had believed in nothing beyond the immediate world. The thin, precarious rind of green.

The memory of that disappointment came back to him, enhanced by the power of the drug. The disappointment itself came back to him, the actual emotion.

'Anyone home?' he shouted at the nearest grave, and had to stop, incapacitated by laughter.

'I know you're *in* there! Yoohoo!'

These words, falsetto, were so funny that he bent almost double, holding his sides. Recovered, he walked on into the outer suburbs of the graveyard, the Dream Home Belt, *Casa Rossi* somewhere among them. Every word that he spoke, every inscription that his gaze discovered seemed sidesplittingly funny. He felt an urge to knock on the horizontal marble door of Beppe's home, and this thought alone was enough to trigger another convulsion.

'Skin and bone!' he shouted, shaking with laughter. 'Put on some meat!'

Gathering himself, he walked on through the spitting rain, his progress punctuated by more shouted asides, and fresh explosions of laughter. *At least you've got a roof over your head! Nice morning for a lie-in. Warm enough down there?*

Each line seemed the most hilarious he had ever heard, let alone uttered, surprising him as if springing from some secret part of his mind, and arriving in his mouth complete, previously undetected. When he repeated the lines, they sounded just as funny, with the power to surprise him all over again.

He found himself standing at his father's grave, as if by accident.

'Still dead, then?' Mack said, and as he stood in the drizzling rain, laughing at this, another joke, the joke of the night, jumped onto his tongue and skidded out in a cloud of vapour.

'Now that,' he shouted, fighting against his own mirth, 'is what I call one hundred fucking percent disability!'

He laughed again, holding his sides, with tears in his eyes, until his legs went weak, and he was forced to slump onto a bench beneath a pepper tree. The joke held its humour, or at least its irony, for some minutes. As he sat, guffawing from time to time, his mind began to clear. The drug was leaching from him; he seemed to be expelling it with each cloudy breath, smoking it out just as he had earlier smoked it in. And with it, slowly, went the last of the jokes. For the first time he shivered, aware of the cold. The rain steadily dimpled the puddles beyond the protectorate of the tree, and leaked through the umbrella of foliage here and there in larger, aggregate drops. Another memory came to him: of running through rain to the pub to fetch his father one wintry pension day. Mack must have been all of ten, perhaps eleven. His father's favourite racer — a tough blue cock, given away as lost, or taken by a falcon, on a race from the Far North weeks before — had appeared, magically, in the narrow trapping passage of the coop. The bird was bedraggled, but fit; the rubber racing-ring intact on its leg. Mack had run immediately to the pub without thinking, fuelled more by his own joy than any need to please his father. The rain had ceased as the two of them emerged from the front bar, but the downpour had filled the potholes and flooded the street gutters. The old man was surprisingly compliant. Beer had lifted him out of his usual morning torpor and self-obsession, but had not yet pushed him beyond his terrible upper threshold. Beer, or the good news from the pigeon-coop, had also healed his war-wounds temporarily. He had handed his walking stick to his son and gripped the boy's shoulder. Somehow balancing on each leg in turn, stork-fashion, he tugged off his big, soft moccasins and planted his bare feet in the nearest puddle.

For a moment he stood there, ankle-deep, then stepped out of the puddle and into the next. And on into the next, wading homewards from puddle to puddle, planting each foot as carefully and exactly as if on stepping stones.

Mack, clutching the walking stick and moccasins, had wanted to run after him, to wrap his arms about him and share whatever he was feeling. At that moment, for the first time in his life, he sensed that the two of them might understand each other, might speak the same language which was the language of boys, the native tongue of the land of Boy.

Could a single good memory redeem the others, the

numberless bad? Clearly not. Emerging slowly from the anaesthesia of booze and dope, he saw one thing with utter clarity: he could only forgive himself if he could forgive his father.

The notion also seemed given to him, surprising him like a joke, or a gift from somewhere outside his normal train of thought. But having thought it, and spoken it, what then? *Detto, fatto:* said, done? If only it was that simple. Sitting near the grave Mack saw this, also: that he had avoided the old man through his last months of life because he had enjoyed seeing him suffer. And this knowledge had been, at some deeper level, unenjoyable, even repulsive. For the first time in his life the invalid was genuinely, seriously ill: his skin and the whites of his eyes slowly yellowing, his flesh wasting away. But still Mack preferred to keep his distance. He knew the forms of behaviour that were required — Lisa reminded him nightly — but found himself unable even to fake the role.

'You're avoiding yourself,' Lisa said. 'Not him.'

The avoidance was easy to explain to his parents, who both denied any problem to the end, and therefore any special need to visit. The changes in his father — the shrivelling, the discolouring— were more obvious to Mack and Lisa, visiting infrequently, than to his mother.

The phone call from his mother reached him at school; it came as no surprise. He arranged for an undertaker to remove the body that same afternoon before visiting her. The funeral could not be so easily avoided, although he pretended until the last minute that he might not attend.

'If I go,' he told a disgusted Lisa, 'it's for Mum, not him. And to make up the numbers.'

His extra number wasn't needed, he was surprised to find. A large crowd of Returned Men, pigeon fanciers and drinking mates, all of them unknown to Mack, was crammed into the pews of the Elizabeth Street church. The priest, never having known the deceased, mouthed the usual second-hand excuses. *The War Changed Him. He Saw Things. He Wasn't the Same.*

'He never came here,' Mack muttered in Lisa's ear. 'He liked to say he wouldn't be seen dead in church.'

'Ssh.'

The young priest opened his Bible and read: '*And again, Noah sent forth the dove out of the ark, and the dove came to him in the evening, and lo, in her mouth was an olive leaf pluckt off …*'

'Uh-oh,' Mack muttered.

'Ssh.'

His suspicions were confirmed as the priest closed the thick book, and looked up over the gathering, less sharing their grief than colluding in it. 'In a sense, we are all God's homing pigeons. And when He calls us back at last, to His loft, we will know that we have come to our own final home …'

Mack was tempted to coo. He left his mother in the front pew with Lisa, and took a walk outside, if only to prevent himself from laughing out loud. Later, at the graveside, he found himself surrounded by solicitous mourners. His amusement had been mistaken for grief.

'A hard act to follow,' someone murmured in his ear.

'Hard shoes to fill,' another agreed.

More stock noises followed. *A terrific mate. One of the best. Funniest bastard I ever knew …*

Who were they talking about? Funeral fibs, certainly, but even allowing for the usual suspension of memory, it was surely someone else they had come to bury. Mack glanced about, recognising almost none of these faces.

'This is the McNeil funeral,' he announced, loudly.

Lisa had a firm grip on his arm. 'Please, Mack. Try to behave. For your mother's sake.'

'It's in the blood,' he said.

'Try to remember the good things.'

He turned on her, and suddenly, from somewhere, perhaps from the same place as his jokes, came the blaze of anger. '*What* good things? I'm glad the cunt is dead!'

Even those words had been forgiven — but not, he now saw, by himself. The words had taken some effort to utter, although their truth was instantly clear to him; something he must have always known, or felt, but discovered only by the act of speaking. Now, years later, as he sat surrounded by falling rain, fresh tears began to fall from his eyes, tears this time without laughter, a flood of grief that was less for his father than for himself, or perhaps for both of them, together. It still felt the same, exactly, as the only time he could ever remember crying, years before, at the funeral of Beppe.

The rain increased its flow again; he rose from the bench and stepped out from beneath the tree. Drenched, but no longer shivering, kept warm, perhaps, by the energy of grief, he turned up his face, and let the freshwater wash the salt from his eyes. And if the cold bite of those drops was in part a punishment, it was also in part, an anaesthetic. It seemed to Mack that the rain was washing him cleaner. Try to be good, Lisa had urged that day, years before, under this very tree. Sound advice — and if trying was merely a kind of acting, or pretence, then perhaps pretending to be good was sufficient. Or pretending at least to be *better.* If the muscles of the face could be retrained by the simple movements of eating, then he could surely smile, unnaturally, until some deep inner wind changed direction and the smile became second nature.

He was shivering again, but that shivering was difficult to distinguish from his usual restlessness. Enough of tears. Enough, too, of thinking. Thoughts were words, and words were cheap. *I fatti contano più delle parole.* The Italian came to him with such clarity that he turned to the phone box, glowing in the distance. Actions speak louder than words.

He knelt at his father's gravestone, and scrubbed at the most recent crusting of birdshit with the wet sleeve of his tracksuit. Pigeon shit? He felt the faint stirring of amusement again. Whatever the substance was, moistened by the rain, it came away easily. Job complete, he stood and walked purposefully out of the dark, sodden cemetery, and crossed the street to his truck.

5

The beating of rain on tin masked the sound of Mack's movement through the shrubbery at the side of the boy's house. He was carrying a carton of milk — an alibi — which he used as a blunt scythe, hacking his way through the wet, overgrown bush. Three windows were set into the single brick wall. The first, small and high and louvred, was clearly no bedroom. Of the others, Shaun's was easy to pick. The flyscreen had long since been removed, and leant against the side of the house; it might have been a weaving-frame, its wire mesh thickly plaited with weeds.

A cement block stood beneath the sill, forming a makeshift step. The boy's description had been accurate: a door.

Mack tapped at the glass pane, softly, then again more loudly. A pale face loomed out of the blackness of the room; the window was raised.

'I thought you might like to earn some pocket money,' Mack whispered.

Shaun's voice was loud, jarring. 'Depends. Delivering milk?'

Mack lowered his own voice even more. 'Furniture moving.'

'How much?'

'Twenty bucks. For an hour.'

'But it's raining.'

'Thirty bucks.'

'You don't need to whisper, Mack.'

'I didn't want to wake anyone.'

The boy hooted, briefly and loudly. 'Fat chance. What if it's longer than an hour?'

'Time and a half after that.'

'Be right there.'

The pale face merged back into blackness; the room exploded silently with light. Mack, leaning on the sill, squinting against the sudden glare, watched as the boy scrounged for clothes. Bunks lined two facing walls, with a narrow walkway between. Three of the four berths were occupied: smaller brothers, sleeping the sound sleep of the pre-pubescent. Makeshift shelves of plank and brick connected bunk to bunk, floor to ceiling. Too many clothes and toys and brothers were crammed into too small a space, but it was a neat sort of congestion. Everything at least had a pigeonhole. The cramped order brought to mind a submarine interior. The air in the room had an underground stuffiness to it, a thick, reeking brew of kerosene heater, nappy solution, last night's stew, and stale beer. Plus the feral, slightly greasy smell of unwashed boy.

It was Mack's childhood cabin, exactly — if with a few extra hands on board. The mix of powerful smells, sweet and sour, pleasant and unpleasant, stirred his memories equally.

The room blacked out again, abruptly; Shaun pushed past him, climbing across the lintel of his high door.

'Where we going?'

'Just around the corner.'

'Can I drive?'

A moment's hesitation. 'Okay.'

He drove well, no novice, even at thirteen or fourteen, but with a clear, childish pleasure. That now familiar mix of innocence and knowledge.

'Double declutch,' he discovered, immediately.

'Antique gear-box,' Mack confirmed.

'Not much guts.'

'It's a milk truck, not a Ferrari. Turn left here.'

The wet streets were empty, the houses still in darkness. Mack peered through the blurred windscreen, past the clockwork scraping of the wipers, seeking landmarks.

'Stop here.'

He climbed down, and jogged, hunched against the drizzle, towards the only lit windows in Edward Street. The front door of the Nursing Home was locked; he pressed his nose to the clear glass pane and peered through into the foyer. No one in sight. He pressed a button marked Night Bell; after some time a voice, female, indistinct, crackled through an intercom.

'Who is it?'

He lowered his mouth to the speaker. 'I've come to see my mother. Mrs McNeil.'

'It's not visiting hours.'

'I was delivering milk,' he said. 'I sleep during the day.'

A pause. 'Wait there.'

A nursing sister appeared in the foyer, middle-aged, pencil-thin, harried-looking. A name tag was clipped to the lapel of her grubby uniform: JEAN, in big print the size of a tabloid headline. She peered suspiciously through the glass pane of the door, keeping her distance even though that door was locked.

Mack combed a hand through his wet, dishevelled hair, but could do nothing about the two-day stubble. He stepped to one side, and gestured towards the milk truck behind him: Exhibit A, proof of solid citizenship. A cigarette tip glowed briefly in the dark cabin.

He bent his head again to the intercom. 'I know it's early, Jean. But it's the only time I can visit. She'll be awake. She's always awake.'

Could he be heard? The nurse, Jean, watched him for a moment longer, deciding. Her eyes were dark-rimmed, the features of her thin face pinched with weariness. A decision was made, perhaps merely the line of least resistance; she stepped closer and unlocked the door.

'Thank you.'

'She's in Room 24.'

He smiled. 'I have been here before.'

'I don't remember your face.'

He swallowed the obvious retort: I don't remember yours.

His mother was lying in her bed. Her eyes were closed, but she was nodding to the radio that murmured softly at her ear. She might have been agreeing with whatever was being said, or merely beating time to music. Mack bent and kissed her forehead; she opened her eyes, startled.

'Paul?' A moment to grasp his presence. 'Is something wrong?'

'Nothing's wrong. I've come to invite you to breakfast.'

'When?'

'Today. Now. And tomorrow, if you like.'

Her eyes searched behind him, as if an explanation might appear in the door.

'Is Lisa with you, dear?'

'In spirit.'

He opened the narrow wardrobe in a corner of the room, and scanned the array of heavy winter dresses.

'What do you want to wear?'

'Is it cold out?'

'Wet. But it's going to be fine.'

'Perhaps the velvet.' Another pause as he laid the dress across her bed. 'It's *very* early, dear.'

'It's late for me, Mum. I've just finished work.'

Her eyes searched his face, her expression guarded. He knew that look: a mix of worry and suspicion, but disguised. She was trying to decide if he was drunk.

'I've taken over a milk round,' he said, in his most sober voice.

'As well as teaching?'

'Instead of teaching.'

He helped her dress as she worried further at this, straightening the dark, heavy velvet over various bulges, without averting his eyes or hands, inuring himself. He commandeered a vacant wheelchair from the corridor, and helped her ease her bulk into the narrow canvas seat, kneeling to adjust the foot rests. The nursing sister was nowhere in sight. He wheeled his mother smoothly out the front door as if moving white goods with a hand-trolley.

'This is Shaun,' he told her at the truck.

'Hello, dear. You help Paul with the deliveries?'

A red cigarette tip was flicked from the driver's window. 'I'm thinking about it.'

Shaun climbed down from behind the wheel, the

two of them helped the big woman up from the wheelchair and into the high cabin.

'Wait here, Mum. We won't be long.'

They returned together to her room. The sister appeared in the door, carrying something in a stainless steel bowl covered with tissue paper.

'I don't understand, Mr McNeil. What do you think you're doing?'

'Taking Mum for an outing, Jean.'

'At this hour? You can't just *take* her. And who's he?'

'Her grandson.'

She stood, glancing from one to the other. Then shook her head, wearily. 'Why *my* shift?'

'Don't worry — I take full responsibility.'

'When will you be bringing her back?'

'When she wants to come back.'

If she wants to come back was implicit, and unspoken — but Jean heard the inflection, clearly. She shrugged, and turned away, too exhausted to care. 'One less mouth to feed, I suppose.'

One less arse to wipe, Mack almost added. He opened out a folded bedspread, a patchwork of crocheted squares, and stacked his mother's other dresses on top, still on their wire hangers, bent double. Next came the contents of various drawers, spilled onto the growing pile. Under instructions, Shaun added the various framed photographs and little china ornaments that were scattered across every horizontal surface in the room. Between them they carried the awkward bundle out to the truck, a makeshift Santa-sack. The rain had eased, but Mack covered the bundle with the waterproof poncho.

His mother watched from the cabin, trying to make sense of events. 'What are you doing, Paul?'

'I thought you might want to stay on a bit, Mum.'

He turned away towards the Nursing Home, but she called him back.

'Dear — it might be nice to be asked.'

The words were a rebuke, if a kind one; his first for many years. She was right; he was taking her assent for granted, treating her like an item of furniture. But the rebuke stirred nothing but pleasure in him: it was a sign of life, and even independence, in that old head.

He reached up a hand and squeezed her forearm, suddenly sentimental.

'I'm calling you in, Mum,' he said.

She understood immediately, and smiled, touched. She too remembered those summer evenings when the pigeons would swoop and wheel high above, and Mack would stand by the loft with a handful of linseed or chunk of bread in his hand. Calling In.

'A pigeon has to *want* to come home,' she said, but still smiling, playing with him, and with the idea.

He re-entered the Nursing Home with Shaun in

tow. The nurse was busy now with paperwork at the high reception counter, ignoring them. Back and forth they moved for the next thirty minutes, carrying out the bedroom furniture, piece by piece, in two hands or four. The room was soon stripped bare, leaving only the high hospital bed, and two framed prints: standard issue flower arrangements and seascapes. Mack took a last glance around. A thermometer poked from a plastic cup attached to the head of the bed, next to the oxygen outlet and nurse call button.

He slipped it into his top pocket.

The sister pushed some sort of discharge form across the reception desk as he passed for the last time. 'Mr McNeil. You have to sign.'

'What is it? A receipt?'

No response. He took the proffered pen, and scribbled on a dotted line. *Received, with thanks, one mother.*

A weak joke, but it brought a glimmer of friendliness from the sister. 'Good luck.'

Shaun was waiting by the truck, bent around the glow of another cigarette as if warming himself by a small fire, while Mack's mother was making small talk at his back.

'I'm sorry to get you out so early …'

Mack scattered a pile of coins from the milk collection bag across the driver's seat, and separated off thirty dollars' worth; a heavy handful.

'No smokes,' he said. 'And no spraypaint.'

A lopsided grin. 'You need a hand at the other end?'

'Lisa will help. You want a lift home?'

Shaun cast an eye at the lightening sky. 'I can walk.' The insolent, likeable grin again. 'Not much room inside.'

'You can ride in the back.'

This time the boy laughed, a brief snort. 'See you tomorrow morning, Mack.'

'If you're there.'

'I'll be there.'

'*Le parole costano poco,*' Mack said, not believing him.

'What's that supposed to mean?'

'Words are cheap.'

'Then why not say it? Since when were you a wog?'

'An honorary wog,' Mack said.

He glanced at his mother. Did the phrase ring bells? Or was she still too preoccupied with her own dislocation to notice? He climbed up into the truck beside her, and pulled the door shut.

'*Buona notte,*' he called through the window, enjoying the echo, but also sending up, in part, the role he found himself playing. All he needed was the eyebrow, drawn with a cartoonist's thick felt-tip, and a tube of *Baci* with its collection of cute mottoes and enigmatic phrases. '*Sogni d'oro.*'

'Fuck you too,' the boy said, grinning, already walking away.

'I'm sorry to cause so much trouble,' his mother said.

He turned to her, suddenly serious.

'No, Mum,' he said. '*I'm* sorry. I'm truly sorry. You should never have been in that shit-hole.'

'It wasn't that bad, dear. I made friends. People with my interests ...'

She was repeating, verbatim, the arguments Mack had used to her, years before, when he had first urged the move.

'You're not going back,' he said firmly, before the words she was chanting persuaded her otherwise, the soothing music of their liturgy deafening her ears to the facts.

She turned her plump, red face towards him. 'I'm not sure what you're doing, dear. I'm not sure *you* know what you're doing. But thank you.'

Tears glistened in her eyes; he turned on the ignition, and clunked the gear-stick roughly into position. 'Don't get sentimental on me Mum. I'm only doing what any son would do.'

6

Next stop was Anthea's, and another calling in. The parallel still amused him, but only to a point; in Lisa's case he wasn't sure who was calling whom, and who was standing by the loft holding the tidbits. He drove up out of the western suburbs and straight through the city centre, following some deep east-west chasm until the high, glass cliff-faces became low-rise again, and he found himself in the inner eastern suburbs, among rows of bluestone cottages and designer townhouses, less Volvo Belt or Range Rover Belt than Hatchback Belt. Anthea's terrace might have been a type of hatchback itself; a doll's house whose roof could be flipped up, and the miniature furnishings lifted out.

The sun may or may not have been up above the Hills; the light, filtered through heavy cloud cover, was still dull, more twilight than daylight. Mack rapped the brass door knocker, waited only a moment, then rapped again.

Muffled footsteps and a faint tinkling from within. The door opened, narrowly. A thin slice of face appeared; a single eye above a taut latch chain.

'She doesn't want to see you, Mack.'

'You wish.'

'Think what you like — it's nothing to do with me. I'm sure she'll contact you when she's ready.'

Anthea moved to close the door, but Mack was quicker: the tip of his toe was firmly wedged.

'I come in peace, Anthea.'

'You've been drinking.'

'Only milk.'

Her smile was reluctant, and exasperated — as much with herself, perhaps, for smiling, as with Mack.

'Please remove your foot, Mack. We don't need a scene.'

'I want to see my wife. I'll remove my foot if you tell Lisa that I'm here.'

'Mack — I need you to remove your foot so that I can open the door.'

He left the foot there a moment longer, not wanting to believe her. Provoked, she raised her voice slightly. 'Do you have any understanding of what you did? This is not something you can joke away, Mack.'

She was right, of course. But something in him continued to rebel. Something made him answer back.

'If I apologise to anyone, Miss Pridmore — it won't be to you.' He raised his voice, calling down the passage, past her. 'Lisa!'

'No need to shout. I'll tell her you're here.'

Released from the opposing pressure of Anthea's weight, the door jerked open another inch, straining. The chain was brass, matching the other door fittings: style winning out over security. Mack removed his foot, worried that the fancy chain would snap. The murmuring of voices carried to him from within, then the approach of different, more familiar steps: a brisk, precise beat of feet on floor, a rhythm he knew by heart. He took the thermometer from his pocket and jammed it between his lips.

Lisa's eye and nose appeared in the gap; she took in the thermometer and shook her head, wearily.

'You can't help yourself, can you?'

But there was hope, he saw: the glimmer of a smile. It spread, slightly.

'You ovulating, Mack?'

He mumbled, through pursed lips, 'Been getting a few hot flushes.'

She snorted. 'Must be the menopause.'

He laughed with her, relieved. The thermometer spilled from his parted lips; he grabbed wildly, juggled it twice, and finally caught it with both hands, cupped.

Lisa unlatched the chain, and opened the door, genuinely amused now — but Mack's smile died. The sight of her cheek, swollen, and discoloured by a yellow bruise, was sobering. The punkish redness had been washed from her hair; the natural colour, a fairish brown, also seemed sobering, or serious.

She stepped through the door and kissed him lightly on the lips.

'I'm pleased to see you, all the same. I shouldn't be — but I am.'

She glanced over his shoulder at the truck in the dark street, and the indistinct moon-face watching from the passenger seat.

'Who's that?'

'Mum.'

'At eight in the morning? You sure you haven't been drinking?' Her nose twitched, a breathalyser, testing the air. 'What's going on, Mack?'

'An abduction.'

She peered into his face, a long, searching examination. 'What is this — some sort of fantasy? One big extended family?'

'Wog Heights must be getting to me,' he said.

This joke brought no response; Lisa was asking for forgiveness, but was not yet ready to forgive him. Not so much for the blow — that transaction was now complete, he sensed — but for other, earlier blows.

'*Vengo con il mio cuore in mano,*' he said.

The corners of her mouth stretched again, tentatively. 'I used to love it when you talked Italian to me,' she said. 'My big fake Latin lover. But what's it mean?'

'I come with my heart in my hand.'

'It's not that simple, Mack.'

'It can start that simple. I'm not taking Mum back. *That's* simple.'

'Is this all for my benefit?'

'Does it matter why — if the result's the same?'

'Maybe not. Or not so much.' She stepped forward and wrapped her arms around him, pressing her face into his chest. 'I *have* missed you.'

'I can't think why.'

She stepped away, smiling through sudden tears. 'You must be a habit.'

He had arrived without words rehearsed. After the events of recent days he knew only that he needed her company; not so much talking to her as just being near her, in her vicinity, and maybe — with luck — touching her. Perhaps she, too, was a habit, but it seemed pointless to speculate too deeply. How suddenly seemed more important than Why.

'I've been doing some thinking,' he said.

She waited, watching his face.

He said, 'I can't work out why you stay with me.'

'I'm *not* with you. I left you, remember?'

But she was smiling, teasing him.

'We're not well-matched, Mack. This marriage was always a bad idea.'

'It seemed like a good idea at the time.'

Once upon a time. On a mountain top, on a wintry day much colder than today. When her smile, despite lips blue with cold, had warmed him, deeply, as it did now. He almost stretched out his hands to the glow.

'There's a whole lot of work to be done, Mack.'

'We can't do it here.'

'Come inside,' she said. 'I'll get my things.'

He followed her into the house. She had been sleeping on a divan in the study; he stood behind her as she packed. Anthea appeared in the doorway.

'Let me guess. You're going back to him?'

'I had to belt her a couple of times,' he said. 'To bring her to her senses.'

'You think that's funny?'

'Please, children,' Lisa intervened. 'Pretend to be friends.'

She turned to her husband. 'It wasn't funny, Mack. Not even slightly. Some of the jokes — I want you to think before you speak.'

'Cut every second joke?'

'Don't go overboard. You still make me laugh. Maybe every third.' She turned to her friend. 'Mack doesn't mean it. He's not like that. Most of the time, anyway.'

I'm really very sensitive, he almost said — but held his tongue, for that would have been the second joke, of sorts, and he had promised.

'I don't know what she sees in you,' Anthea said, wearily, but without malice, as if willing to be persuaded otherwise.

My big thick cock, he almost told her, but held his tongue again. That would have been the third joke, which meant he was now in credit; but as they drove away, Lisa, his mother, and himself, squeezed across the bench of the truck, more jokes were beyond him. The exhilaration that had powered him through the morning's calling in — to Shaun's window, to the Nursing Home, and on to Anthea's — was wearing off, like a drug high. He felt overwhelmingly tired.

'One thing we have to get straight,' Lisa was saying. 'You're too hard on Anthea. I don't have many friends. I want you to respect the friends I have.'

'Will you make the same speech to her?'

'I have.'

'It didn't seem to work.'

'She listens to me. Which is more than I can say for you.'

'She loves you,' Mack said.

'I love *her*. She has qualities you refuse to allow yourself to see.'

They were speaking across the central bulk of Mack's mother, silent up to that point. For the first time she opened her mouth.

'He's always had a mind of his own,' she told her

daughter-in-law. 'Just like his father.'

'Stubborn as a mule,' the younger woman agreed, then leaned forward, speaking again to Mack. 'Which reminds me — you know the reason you don't like Anthea?'

'Gee, let me guess,' he said. 'I'm just like her, too?'

'You have the same sense of humour.'

'Peas in a pod,' he said. *'Due gocce d'acqua.'*

The women exchanged glances.

'That's another thing, Mack,' Lisa said. 'The Italian can be fun. But you go overboard. It's like the jokes — you never know when to stop.'

'Non è vero!' he said, automatically. *'È impossibile!'*

Lisa reached awkwardly past her mother-in-law and pressed her hand across his mouth. 'Don't be a pain.'

'Scrap every third phrase?' he mumbled.

She released the pressure on his lips. 'Every second.'

They fell silent. His mother apologised for a red light; Mack let the apology pass without interruption or irony. Waves of weariness were washing over him, ever higher and stronger. Doubts were also beginning to surface. The idea of rescuing the two women had seemed, like his marriage, a good idea at the time — a fairy tale fantasy. The idea, and the acting on it, had been the easy part. It was, simply, not that simple.

A disturbing thought: did the consequences of his precipitate actions now, in fact, have to be spoken of in words? Worked through, sorted out — *solved*? Or could those consequences be addressed by further action, later? The hands of the dashboard clock were nearing nine o'clock. For the moment, it was best to look no further ahead than that.

'What time you due at school?'

'It's Saturday, Mack.'

He tried to absorb this astonishing fact into his weary brain. Saturday, the sporting Sabbath, and he hadn't noticed.

7

To surrender to sleep was not yet possible. He backed the truck to the top of the drive, assisted his mother inside, then unloaded the furniture via the terrace, carrying each piece straight through the French windows into the largest of the spare rooms or using the wheelchair when necessary. Lisa helped with the heaviest items; his mother spent an hour or so making up the spare bed, and the rest of the morning recovering from the effort, lying on top of it, breathless. Hunger laid claim to Mack's attention towards noon; he searched the kitchen thoroughly but could find nothing but a pair of end-crusts in a plastic bag of sliced bread.

As he rummaged in the cupboards, Lisa appeared, pausing in the doorway, headed towards the spare room with a stack of towels and face washers. 'What's for breakfast?'

'Toasted book-ends. Where's Mum?'

'Still in bed. Too much excitement for one day.'

'My feelings exactly. Feel like breakfast in bed?'

Her eyes found his, an unspoken understanding; she moved on, out of frame.

He dropped the two crusts into the toaster, then checked on his mother. She was lying on the made bed and her radio was murmuring, but she seemed to be sleeping. The smell of burnt toast summoned him away, at speed. He scraped the outer coating of soot into the sink, and spread the brittle remnants with butter, then with peanut butter, the only ointments he could find. The two butters seemed to possess healing properties, rejuvenating the burnt surfaces and restoring, at least partially, suppleness to the bread. He filled the teapot and carried various offerings — tea, milk, partly-healed toast — on a tray into the bedroom.

Lisa was waiting beneath the quilt; a pink scarf shrouded the glowing bedlamp. After eating, they nestled together for a time amid the crumbs, content to listen to the steady, continuing beat of rain on roof, and the gush of water in the gutters and downpipes. At length, she leant over and kissed him on the mouth, an invitation as tender as any *Bacio*. They came together immediately, with a pleasure made even more extreme by their time apart.

'So you've forgiven me too?' she asked as they lay entangled afterwards.

She had already forgiven him, she was saying, but it was the literal question that jarred his sleepy mind; he would have preferred no reminder of her pregnancy, however oblique. He had avoided thinking of it in her absence. He had missed her too much to think about it. But he knew the wound remained. As did the cause of its discovery: his infertility. His knee, his wrist, his balls — the parts of his body seemed to be acting together, a conspiracy, to betray him. But he felt stronger now, above all that. His head — his mind — was still intact, and able to quell those mutinous parts, or at least ignore them.

'You were drunk,' he said. 'It wasn't you.'

The words were still to some extent a formula, a mask, but he spoke with some firmness, wanting to sign off the conversation. For now, the correct action was to act as if it had never happened. And this seemed to gel his tired thoughts, or shift them towards some sort of conclusion. To act is to be? Even this simple sentence — a formula itself, a string of single syllables — seemed too complex for his weary mind to grasp. But the feelings behind the words, the rough mix of feeling and thinking that preceded speaking, might well have taken those names and labels if given time enough.

'I was under an anaesthetic,' she said.

'He laughed, softly and briefly. If so, he felt no urgent need to know that different, anaesthetised self.

'We'll have to move,' he said, changing the subject. 'We can't stay here forever.'

'We'll manage,' Lisa said. 'We'll find a place.'

'A *big* place,' he murmured drowsily.

She slipped from the bed, leaving him to sleep. He

lay in the residue of her musk, breathing her warm, woman smell, his mind drifting between sleep and dream. In that half-conscious mid-state, his thoughts lost their usual definition, their colours running together, swimming in and out of focus. Old associations broke apart, new connections were suddenly possible: odd, unlikely inspirations. One such struck him: the decision — the choice — to play a role was already a fulfilment of the role, was already something *deeper* than the role. The notion was a little confused in his mind, and still elusive; he tried to concentrate to narrow the focus.

The act of choice itself was a change for the better?

It was also a beginning — and if the rest of his ruminations came to nothing in the light of day, this last thought, at least, was satisfying. His sleepy mind nestled among such notions, snug as wrapped chocolate. He had arrived, after much booze, sweat and tears, at a string of comforting clichés, perhaps — but they were no less useful, or even true, for that. His eyes closed at last.

The rain drummed its soft percussive brushes against the roof. After a few bars of that music — the music of sleep, half-silence — he slept.

And slept on through the afternoon, and well into the night. His bladder woke him at two, some hours before the radio alarm. Lisa was back beside him, sleeping; he slipped quietly from beneath the quilt and stood, pissing, in the cold bathroom. After shaking the last drops from the tip of his cock, he filled his shaving mug with hot water, whisked up a lather, and slapped it onto his chin and cheeks with broad, careless brushstrokes. The shaving itself was a different matter; he scraped with painstaking care, and the face that emerged from the soapy mask looked younger or at least more carefully carved than it had for some time. There was a sense of ceremony in this, a conscious ritual, that seemed important.

He slid open the French windows and stepped through onto the terrace, still naked. Almost time for the milk round. Automatically, he sought out the Club lights in the distance; of course they would not be burning at two in the morning. But this seemed somehow propitious, and satisfying, as if that part of his life, that powerful incandescence, had been extinguished for good. He knew that he would never play again, but the realisation did not seem terrifying. It had stolen over his brain like sleep, perhaps during sleep, becoming a certitude almost without him noticing. Perhaps he would race pigeons instead. Perhaps not.

'Shut the door,' Lisa's blurred voice called from inside.

He slid the door shut behind him, remaining outside. The noise of rain on the roof had been deceptive: amplified, like drumming on a sounding-board, or wings beating against the walls of a dove-cote. The amount of drizzle was hardly discomfiting: the brief, pinpoint agony of each drop was so sharp and cold that the naked skin was immediately anaesthetised, as if by a tiny frostbite.

A small van laboured up the hill, and stopped below the house. A shadowy figure emerged, hurried to the end of the drive, then back again to the van: the local milkman, an early riser, bringing his litre of coals to Newcastle. Mack moved further onto the terrace, into the drizzle, and descended the wide marble steps to the driveway. At the foot of the stairs he stepped accidentally into a puddle, and then, deliberately, sprang into another, some distance away, and again into another — suddenly determined, perversely, to reach the far end of the drive without leaving the freezing water. This simple task seemed important, although he wasn't sure how the world might change if he failed. His slow, jerky ballet, a series of dance-steps dictated by the position of the puddles, brought him at last to the end of the drive; he stooped and grasped the single carton firmly, as if it were a baton. It was his turn, *this* him, the man he now was, to carry that baton a little further. But as he straightened, as naked as when he first entered the world, he seemed, for the moment, to have travelled forward far enough in time; he had paused, temporarily, on a kind of landing, a little older and a little wiser.

MAESTRO

Against the backdrop of Darwin — that small,
tropical hothouse of a port, half-outback, half-oriental, lying at
the tip of North Australia — a young and newly arrived
southerner encounters the 'maestro', a Viennese refugee with a
shadowed past. The occasion
is a piano lesson, the first of many . . .

*'A beautifully crafted novel dealing with the tragic gulf between talent
and genius; between the real and the spurious.'*
C. J. Koch

Shortlisted
Miles Franklin Award

ISBN 0207 189323

HONK IF YOU ARE JESUS

A 'scientific romance' in the tradition of H. G. Wells?
An Orwellian satire? From the pen of Peter Goldsworthy — a
modern champion of the lost art of storytelling — comes a
novel that resists categorisation and explodes expectations.

*'Subtly symphonic . . . Dazzlingly imaginative . . . it wouldn't surprise
me if this novel came to share a place with books such as* The Loved
One *or* Brave New World.*'*
Les Murray, *Sydney Review*

A *Times Literary Supplement*
International Book of the Year 1993

ISBN 0207 189315

LITTLE DEATHS

In a gripping novella, 'Jesus Wants Me For a Sunbeam', and nine
accompanying bittersweet short stories, Peter Goldsworthy
explores the edges of death.

*'Probably the most stylish of our writers. His work is distinguished by
elegance, by sharpness of observation, by nicely judged ironies . . . These
pieces are, without exception, marvellously shaped, often wry epiphanies.'*
Andrew Riemer, *Sydney Morning Herald*

Shortlisted
NSW Premier's Awards, Christina Stead Prize
Steele Rudd Award
South Australian Festival Awards

ISBN 0207 189307

WISH

An entrancing and strikingly original love story which explores
the relationship between animals and humans. Born to deaf
parents, John James ('JJ') has always been more at home in Sign
language than in spoken English. A teacher of Sign, he forms a
friendship with the beautiful and highly intelligent 'Eliza'.

'Stylish, imaginative, poignant and hugely unsettling'
Penelope Nelson, *Australian*

*'A deeply satisfying book. . . Represents a new achievement in his
fiction. . . Read it. You won't find another like it.'*
Chris Wallace-Crabbe, *Adelaide Review*

ISBN 0207 189110

IF, THEN

This new poetry collection continues Goldsworthy's exploration
of the natural and philosophical worlds, with extended
sequences of poems on numbers and on colours. *If, Then* also
includes songs from Goldsworthy's libretto for the opera of Ray
Lawler's play, *The Summer of the Seventeenth Doll.*

*'His stylishly chiselled poems offer rueful ironies at the expense of the
universe . . . In every line the poet strives to make language elegant
enough to do justice to the world as comedy.'*
Oxford Companion to Twentieth Century Poetry

ISBN 0207 190178